An Adirondack Escape

That night, Wallace Klocks crossed the paved Lincoln Pond Road running into the fields and woods, down the remnants of a logging road until he could no longer look back over his shoulder and see the dim outline of Moriah Shock. He slipped farther into the woods, startled two grouse, and slowed at a large beech tree carved with initials. He stopped there, panting with his head down, his hands against the smooth bark. He put his arm through the strap of his Nike bag, pushed off and trotted along a sandy path made by all-terrain vehicles.

He avoided a depression, sloped in front of him, but steeper elsewhere. Near the edge, he carefully stepped around coils of thick, two-inch cable, half-buried in the earth. He veered off for another twenty yards, until he saw bushes slanted downwards, and the ground underneath severely undercut. Again, he backed off from the edge of another drop-off, tripping over three sturdy bolts sticking up out of the ground, probably once used to secure cable.

Wary of these uncharted sinkholes, he activated his mind's eye to recall the details of the aerial photographs in Warden A. D.'s office. Raising his knees and placing each foot straight down, he marched in slow motion in the direction of the disappearing horizon of THE 21 MINE.

THE
21 MINE

all the best :)

Jeffrey G. Kelly

[signature: Jeffrey G. Kelly]

Creative Bloc Press
Saratoga Springs, NY

FIRST EDITION, JULY 2000
SECOND PRINTING, FEBRUARY 2001
THIRD PRINTING, APRIL 2004

Published in the United States by Creative Bloc Press
Saratoga Springs, New York

Printed by Sheridan Books, Inc.
Chelsea, Michigan

Distributed by North Country Books, Inc.
Utica, New York

The author wishes to acknowledge the book, *Through the Light Hole,* by Patrick
Farrell, borrowed from the Sherman Free Library in Port Henry, as a valuable
reference for the history of iron ore mining in Essex County, New York.

ISBN: 0-9663423-1-3

Library of Congress Catalog Card Number: 98-92721

For my family

Linda, Spencer and Faber

Acknowledgments

I'd like to thank my three New York readers who functioned as editors and gave me valuable feedback: John Stacey of Greenfield, Sue Kelly of Southhampton, and Marcy Neville of Keene Valley.

My wife, artist Linda Smyth designed the cover. John McPherson gave the figure a 'close to home' right hand, and Susana Dancy enhanced the cover on the computer. Eric Sanborn, with whom I share an office, snapped the photo of me for the back cover. Nancy Butcher and the rest of the Creative Bloc were also helpful in putting up with my picayune grammatical questions throughout this year-long project.

During the research phase of this book, I visited the Mt. McGregor Correctional Facility in Wilton and the Moriah Shock Incarceration Correctional Facility in Mineville. Superintendent Pedro Quinones at McGregor and administrator Lawrence Sterns at Moriah were generous with their time, and I respect the work they do. I would also like to tip my hat to all correctional officers.

AUTHOR'S NOTE

This book is a work of fiction, though the genesis for this story is real. An inmate from Moriah Shock did escape down into the 21 Mine. He was never found.

Before I began writing, I ventured into the nasty, crater-like 21 Mine as far as the cavernous tunnel openings at the bottom. Much of my description of the escape is based on that exploration.

Remember, all the characters in this novel are fictional products of my imagination. Any likeness to real individuals is purely coincidental.

THE
21 MINE

An Adirondack Escape

one

No one bothered them. The short drive from Moriah Shock to Heidi Beauvais's ranch was a chance for the inmates to sightsee and talk quietly. The green van, license plate MOR 12, made a right turn at the prison's carved wooden sign more reminiscent of Woodstock than Mineville. Across the road a fading 1953 blue Pontiac sat tucked in among the fir trees.

The view of the forests and mountains was changing, becoming less like Siberia. The spring of 1999 had melted the snow along with the prisoners' animosity toward the place. They traveled a mile on Lincoln Pond Road past an historical marker before slowing for their work site.

The van turned in the gravel driveway, cruising slowly by the main house where Heidi and her grown daughters lived and got dressed each morning. And this was morning, so all eyes were glued to the house hoping for a glimpse of one of the gypsy daughters.

Near the barn, Inmates Wallace Klocks and Damian Houser stepped off the van and gazed at the horse fields. The sight transfixed Damian. If he could send one postcard from Upstate to the big city, this would be it; horses clustered in the center of a high mountain meadow, their moist breath mixing with the mist.

But where Damian saw poetry, Klocks wondered why? Why were the horses together in the same spot? He asked Billy.

Billy was unscrewing his steel thermos of hot lemon tea. He stopped and looked from the yearlings in the center of the paddock back to Klocks.

"Well Mr. Klocks, I'll tell you this. For some reason, they're standing there on the hottest days of the summer, too." Let him ponder that, Billy thought.

"Maybe it's the shade of the trees?" Klocks probed.

"Maybe," Billy replied. "Move," Billy commanded. "Grab your tools. There are plenty of holes to be dug." Technically, correction officers weren't supposed to talk with inmates, but outside the facility each guard set his own tone. Billy's credo was one of live and let live. Make his day pleasant and he'd tolerate a lot. Basically, Billy was a happy guy, whether he was riding his horse on the ski slopes of Otis Mountain, or scanning packages mailed to Moriah Shock.

Slowly, the six inmates grabbed the picks, shovels, and pry bars, and stepped over the fence posts lying on the ground on the way to their designated holes. Klocks snatched the last pair of leather gloves from the back of the green pick-up.

Klocks' sense of curiosity and his peculiar prescient sense were on alert. Something about this ranch, he thought. His fingers were tingling as if he were dealing the final hand of a high-stakes poker game. Was he chilled, or was it this place and those horses?

Damian was busy lining up the posts, sighting them so they would be perpendicular and in a straight line. It was the best work detail on the crew, since it got him away from digging and filling holes.

For each post hole, the prisoners broke the dirt with a pick ax, and then shoveled down three feet. They would use the pry bars to dislodge the rocks or hardened clay and the post hole digger to dig and extract the dirt. The post hole digger was made of two small shovels attached like scissors. Ram it down into the hole, squeeze the wooden handles together like an accordion, pull up and you had your clump of dirt.

"Almost like clamming on Fire Island," Randy said. "Lot of queers down there."

"Shut up," Billy ordered. He was growing tired of his crap. Naturally, when prisoners are sticking hard posts into holes in the ground a lot of sexual imagery pops up, but Billy let it be known he didn't want to hear "any stupid-ass, sexual jokes."

The 21 Mine

The posts cost six bucks each, pressure treated, with a warranty for thirty years. Stapled to one end was an indestructible tag from a coastal lumber company in Havana, Florida.

"Chromated copper arsenate." With surprising ease, Damian read aloud those tiny words on the bottom of the green tag. "Do not burn, treated wood," he continued, squinting in the morning sun.

"Hey, there's arsenic in these things. Poison." Randy announced.

"Back to work. Let's go," Billy said calmly.

Randy had a face like a hawk and he was a talker and an entertainer. Though his jabber was annoying, the inmates and guards generally put up with him. Randy helped pass the time. A lot of his chatter was the energy of a trapped animal coming out in words. Because Randy was white, because he came from Upstate and was in for DWI, an offense the beer-drinking guards could relate to, they tolerated him and cut him some slack.

Randy rattled on about the great time he had with two college girls down south on a beach at Alligator Point in the Florida Panhandle. The girls were later found murdered.

"Smugglers unloaded cocaine from fishing boats right onto those beaches. That's what happened. The babes were in the wrong place at the wrong time," Randy said with a smirk. "Was that you Klocks? That's one you got away with, right?"

"Shut up, asshole. Unlike you, I don't kill little girls," Klocks said. Usually, no one challenged Klocks. He was a loner and the word was he had connections. Klocks was powerful through his thick chest and wide shoulders, and his eyes were special, marbled green and brown, capable of disarming a foe or deceiving a friend.

Billy's eyes were on Klocks. Billy stepped back a few more paces, raised his club waist high, and warned, "That'll do it, boys. It's Friday. We got to finish today."

* * * *

The fence they were building was in the foothills of the Adirondack Mountains. When the prisoners leaned on their shovels and picks and took in the view of Lake Champlain and the Green Mountains of Vermont, they grew wistful.

Randy had his hand atop one of the fence posts, waiting for instructions. "Ever climb a mountain, Damian?" Randy asked.

"Oh yeah, you betcha," Damian lied. "To the right. Back a little; that's it," He said, guiding Randy.

Damian was different from the rest of the black inmates. The word was he didn't belong. Shouldn't be in prison. Lean, graceful and handsome, he had the face of a Cassius Clay and the aura of an Arthur Ashe. Underneath this ennobling exterior, he was a boy, twenty-two years old, scared about prison, scared about being inside.

He remembered on the bus ride up thinking he hadn't committed a crime, yet here he was in with all these criminals. He had never run with a gang and now he probably had to sell his soul to one. One tear had squeezed out of one eye, and he was deathly afraid that another inmate had witnessed that. Now, after five months, that phase was well buried.

Randy held his post upright and steady while Klocks shoveled bluish gray, chipped stone down into the hole around the post. Once it was secure, Randy let go and tamped the stone with the chiseled end of the pry bar, until it was packed as firm as pavement. Klocks and the others shoveled dirt on top, and more stone and then with the flattened end of the six foot pry bar, again tamped all around the post.

The men took pride in setting a proper horse fence, and they labored hard and argued loudly on where to start the holes for the sweeping curves in the fence. Damian had the final say. "To the left, to the left. That's it, there."

"Why is it that no matter how carefully I pile the dirt next to a hole, there's never enough to fill it back up?" Randy asked out loud to no one in particular.

After tamping the crushed stone, Chico, catching his breath, thinking of an incident down in the city, said to Giovanni for probably the fourth time, "For yourself only and not give me nothin'? That's bullshit. Yourself only!"

The 21 Mine

Giovanni was busy fantasizing about the tits of an ex-girlfriend. He plunged the bar down into the soil and stone in the hole around his arsenic-laden, pressure-treated fence post. Finally he remembered her name and mumbled "Hoochie Mama." Giovanni hardly ever spoke, and for a few moments, the other prisoners were noticeably silent.

"Hoochie Mama?" Randy repeated loudly, leering at Giovanni. Giovanni, six feet four, crowbar in hand, stared back at Randy. Giovanni was usually well-behaved, but Randy didn't quite have a read on the big fellow yet, so he didn't press it. He didn't say "Hoochie Mama" again.

"Damian, move the truck up," Billy commanded. The rusted, pick-up was full of the bluish-gray stone from the mines, called tailings.

"Yo, the sun feels good, don't it," Chico said to Giovanni.

Billy checked his watch, seeing how close they were to lunch. They were having warm weather for April, and some of the inmates were working in their white T-shirts, their green shirts hanging on the posts they had set. Billy looked out beyond the men. Working on a mountain ranch with the lake shimmering in the distance was a beautiful setting. If only the winters weren't so long.

Damian took as much time as he dared backing up the truck. Inmates weren't supposed to drive any vehicles, but Billy recognized that Damian worked hard and besides, he was due to be released in one week. Damian appreciated the privileged detail. The motor was doing all of the work, and you could imagine you were on lunch break in the Islands waving to the ladies out strolling in Old Town.

He stuck his head out of the window and asked Billy. "How's this?"

"Fine, shut her off."

Damian tossed him the keys, which Billy caught easily with his left hand. Billy used to be the best point guard on Elizabethtown's basketball team, the one that went to the Class D state finals. Their team was all white, and the Syracuse team was all black. That's always the way it seemed to Billy, black versus white. Working at the prison was reinforcing that.

Billy felt lucky to have a job close to where he grew up. Most of his friends in the industry were downstate, trying to build up seniority, so they could be transferred back Upstate to a prison in the Adirondacks. After all, Billy was

making more money, thirty-eight thousand dollars, than any of his friends from
his high school graduating class, even the few who had stuck out college. He
kept reminding himself that his salary was pretty damn good, especially for up
here, where guys regularly went on unemployment for the winter, dragging their
shanties out to ice fish on the lake.

The Lake Champlain Bridge glittered in the morning sun like a silver
bracelet. From the running board of the pick-up, Damian stared at the bridge and
the lake and thought about fishing. He had heard the guards talking about
catching large mouth bass in the weeds of Bulwagga Bay. That sounded pretty
good. He could see himself speeding around in one of those bass-fishing boats in
search of a large mouth, zipping across the lake to Vermont. He could travel a
long way in one of those bass-fishing boats.

He stopped daydreaming. Life could be worse, he told himself. The prison
here was better than he ever imagined. It didn't have all the stuff they had in
maximum, like cable and conjugal visits, but the boot-camp training supplied a
regimen of work and honesty, and no idle time for others to come after you. And
most of all, if you didn't quit, you got out early.

The drawback to Upstate was the distance from home. Every other Sunday,
the men were allowed visitors. But for your mom or wife or girlfriend to take a
seven-hour bus ride from Manhattan's Port Authority up here to the cold, was
asking a lot. With so many new prisons in the Adirondacks, occasionally visitors
actually got off at the wrong prison. Damian shuddered thinking about the
nearby prison at Dannemora. Maximum security, home to Son of Sam, New
York City's most famous serial killer.

Klocks dragged over another post and quickly figured out which was the
butt end, picking up the heavy eight footer, and plopping it down in the hole,
leaving about five feet showing. Some of the prisoners preferred working inside
the facility at the wood shop making canoe seats out of cane, but Klocks liked to
be outside to learn the lay of the land.

"How high is the bridge?" Damian asked.

"Just under a hundred feet," Klocks said.

Klocks had read about the bridge in the prison library. Officially, the bridge
was ninety-two feet high. It connected the ruins of His Majesty's Fort at Crown

The 21 Mine

Point with Chimney Point, and on a larger scale the Adirondacks of New York with the Green Mountains of Vermont. Apart from its historic location and construction, the bridge was a thing of beauty. Rays from the rising and setting sun reflected off the center arch and its truss of riveted steel, and at night the bridge lights were a friendly glow in the surrounding darkness. Locally, it was called the Crown Point Bridge, but on postcards and maps it was the Champlain Bridge. To the villagers of Port Henry sitting on their porches on a northern bluff, the eighteen hundred feet bridge was a reassuring sight that some things don't change.

Billy looked from the view, to the paddock, to his watch. All in all, it was a great morning. The last post was set. "Break. Put the tools in the truck bed. You got half an hour."

Everyone sat. Randy passed out oranges to those who wanted them. Klocks took two. He liked fruits with protective skins, and shied away from meats, particularly red meat, which most prisoners craved. The rest of the crew was busy lighting up their smokes. But Klocks didn't smoke cigarettes, didn't smoke pot, even on the outside; didn't do cocaine, and didn't drink alcohol. He was rare that way - careful about what he put in his system, never taking drugs, looking down upon those who did.

While the others sprawled out on the matted hay blowing smoke rings and telling stories, Klocks threw a few karate punches, which annoyed everyone, including Billy, who told him to cool it. Like many prisoners, Klocks was a physical guy and he practiced karate every evening in the squad bay before lights-out, grunting as he executed his flying roundhouse kick. Karate came in handy in prison, where weapons were hard to come by. Even a Latin King gang member carrying a shiv made from a spoon might have second thoughts about messing with you.

While Klocks was kicking and grunting, Randy was staring at a foal grazing in a pasture. He said, "I never thought I'd be building fences and eating pizza in prison."

Billy strolled away from the inmates thinking that this paddock would be large, at least ten acres. Once the paddock fence was finished, the encircling weedy road would be converted to a gravel and dirt track. Heidi planned to exercise the horses on this makeshift track. Billy boarded two of his own horses at Heidi's ranch in hopes of harness racing one day down in Saratoga, the August place to be. Every guard had his dream.

After lunch, phase two would begin. The rails would go up and they would be nailed to the outside of the posts. Ordinarily, rails were nailed to the inside of the posts, so the horses in the corral wouldn't knock the rails off by kicking or chewing against them, both of which they did. But since horses here were also going to be running on a track outside and around this paddock, the rails would be nailed to the outside of the posts, so the horses wouldn't get hurt.

Billy turned and shouted, "Let's go, rail time."

Nobody stirred.

"Eyeballs!" Billy yelled in an unusually harsh manner.

"Snap sir, Snap sir," they responded with varying levels of enthusiasm.

"Get going and distribute the rails around the fence posts. Move it. Damian, you do the math. Get to work, Randy!" Billy barked. "Grab a rail. You'll be holding them level, while I use the nail gun."

For three hours the work progressed smartly. Come late afternoon the men started to lollygag. A few of the men closed their eyes and looked to the sun, coveting the warming rays.

"There's them horses again," Klocks said.

Damian, who had been making sure each rail was set level and parallel, remarked, "You da man," mocking Klocks.

"You're sending me to get water," Klocks directed. "There's water on the other side of the paddock, and the shortest way there is across the field, right by the aspen trees. I'll owe you one."

Damian had heard that Klocks owing you a favor was not a bad thing. Damian tossed him the plastic thermos to fill up at the spigot across the track.

Klocks walked off, attracting Billy's attention.

"Klocks!" Billy yelled.

"Getting water, sir. Damian told me to."

Billy looked to Damian, who sheepishly gestured in the affirmative by shrugging his shoulders.

The 21 Mine

Billy, who still held the nail gun, reluctantly waved Klocks on, as if it were no big deal.

Only two horses stood in the speckled sunlight under the glittering aspens next to the granite boulder. They trotted off as Klocks walked closer. The trees didn't really give that much shade. He slowed as he stepped between the trees and around the one boulder. He felt it before he saw it - cold air blowing up from the ground. He walked onwards to fill the thermos and reached down to pick up two pebbles from the dirt track. On the way back, with Billy watching from afar, he slowed again at the cluster of aspens, and tossed the pebbles in the hole. The pebbles clattered around, falling far underground, as he walked away all ears.

"Bring the water to me," Billy ordered.

Billy took a swig. "Quite a breeze out there, eh Klocks? If you were a horse you'd hang out there in the summer too. Okay, make sure all the men get a drink."

* * * *

Billy used a gun to nail the six hundred rails into the fence posts. The nail gun had a safety device which prevented it from releasing a nail unless the machine made contact at its tip. For instance, if anyone pointed the orange, nail gun in the air at somebody and tried to pull the trigger, it wouldn't fire. Yet it was a kick to use, because the tool gave the guard who used it a sense of power.

Of all the guards to fire the nail gun, Billy could reload the fastest. He wore a meshed vest, its wide pockets strategically stuffed with clips of nails and butane cartridges for fuel. Inmates held the railings in place along the snap lines, one railing running the sixteen foot distance of three posts, while Billy repeatedly pulled the trigger. At least one of the four railings was staggered to tie in and overlap the next group of three posts. As long as the railings had been slid off the pickup at the proper intervals, a good crew of three inmates and one guard could put railings up at the pace of a slow walk.

"Right there, no, no. Up, up, up," Damian said as Randy raised the sixteen foot rail a half inch, which wasn't easy, since it was already nailed into the two preceding posts. "Pa-boom, pa-boom, pa-boom," Billy shot three, coated, three

9

and a quarter inch, twelve-penny nails into the last post. The men were focused on what they were doing, lost in the rhythm of the work. Momentarily, Randy, Damian and Billy felt like equals, laborers doing a job they were quietly proud of.

Using a Stanley hand saw, Randy rushed to saw the few inches off one end of the railing before Billy nailed the end to the middle of the post, leaving room for the next rail, nine nails to a rail, from fifteen to twenty-one nails to a post. When nailing the top rail, Billy held his elbow high, tilting the gun down, and shot the top nail in at an angle. That way when Chico and Esteban sawed off the top of the posts at an angle, so water would run off, they wouldn't clip the nail. In his quest for speed, Billy had to concentrate to remember about that top nail.

It was one of the few times Billy couldn't worry about supervising the inmates. The crew relished this final phase of putting up the fence, because the project was about done, and much like masons admiring their stone work, the prisoners realized that this fence with its pressure-treated posts guaranteed for thirty years, would be there after some of them were dead. They looked back at the line of fencing, and the field of grass it encompassed and made quirky faces to each other, surprised that they had actually done this themselves.

"Jesus, man that fence looks good," Randy said as he shrugged his shoulders. Beyond their fence, they could see the yearlings and stallions that would be shifted to this, the largest of all the paddocks. For a while, some of the inmates forgot they were in prison, and felt like ranchhands, pleased with a job well done.

Billy stepped back and surveyed the fence swerving around the curve in an orderly fashion. Damian's eye for design and proportion, which he had inherited from his art-director father, had been put to good use. Randy gazed beyond the posts, past the aspens, to the ranch. All three of them were waiting for a daughter to saunter out. In their dreams tonight, Damian thought.

"An inch higher," Billy said, while he inserted another butane cartridge into his nail gun. The gun's warning light had been blinking red, indicating that it was low on fuel. Billy tossed the empty fuel cartridge into the bed of the pick-up. Randy scooped it up, and gave the nozzle a few healthy sniffs, feeling high and dizzy for ten seconds.

The 21 Mine

"Just like airplane glue," Randy said smiling and rolling his eyes at Billy, who shook his head in disgust.

"Get back to work. I don't think you got but three brain cells left."

After they nailed the last rails on, Damian slowly drove the pick-up on the makeshift road around the fence, and from a kneeling position in the truck, Chico and Esteban pushed and pulled on a two-man bucksaw to cut the tops of the posts at an angle even with the top rail.

Jeff Kelly

two

B illy looked across the field, startled to see the long, purplish skirt of Chantal moving his way. The prisoners hadn't caught sight of her yet. Why in hell was she wearing a skirt? He cursed. Is she stupid or what? Is she trying to tease the prisoners? Or she's coming to see me? Come on sweetheart, get with it. Maybe her mom thought the Warden was here. Sometimes he wondered about Heidi and her clan. They were out there.

"Shit, boys. Look what's comin'," said Randy, who was still fumbling with one of Billy's empty butane cartridges. The whole crew stopped and the inmates stood straight, watching a woman walking toward them, her skirt swaying with each step.

"I want it all. She knows what she wants," Chico said shuffling his feet to some internal rap beat.

"Who asked you?" Giovanni said.

In this setting, the sight was unexpected. Had they been pouring sidewalks outside the Essex County Court House in Elizabethtown, the inmates knew gawking at the women would be a bonus. But here in a mountain meadow it was unexpected. She moved toward them like a shimmering mirage.

The closer she got the more the details stood out. She had hair down to her ass. She was carrying a basket. She was wearing red Tony Lama cowboy boots, and under her white peasant blouse, they imagined her tits. The prisoners didn't take their eyes off her.

13

"Oh, my heavenly God," Damian said, standing up on the running board of the pick-up.

Billy removed the clip of nails and leaned the gun against a pressure-treated post. None of the crew was working; all were motionless. Chantal was close now, walking around the paddock. As she turned, they watched her reach across and slide her hand down the angled top of one of the newly-sawed fence posts.

Admiring my work, Chico thought.

Billy reasoned that if he yelled at them to get back to work, they wouldn't obey. So he shut up. Never give a command you can't enforce - it only weakens your position, erodes your authority. He reached down and removed the butane cartridge.

Walking a few steps toward her, and away from the inmates, Billy punted a sawed-off post inside the paddock fence.

She was aware that the men were leering at her, and she was determined not to blush. As if answering Billy, she kicked a couple of chunks of post tops away from the weeded road.

Billy turned back to his crew and broke the silence. "No cat calls boys, I know her."

Randy smirked and said, "You've been holding out on us Billy. That ain't right. And you a married man." The rest of the crew chuckled, except for Damian, who was fixated on her dark arms cradling the basket.

Could she be mixed race, a mulatto? No time for any analytical review. His eyes searched her clothes for her figure, her face for her lips, her hair for its color. He took a hundred snapshots.

"Hey Billy," she said as casually as she could muster, stopping about fifteen feet short of Billy and the crew. "Heidi and I were baking cookies, and we're so thankful for the work you all are doing."

She glanced at the faces of the men, at Randy and Damian standing just behind Billy. They all seemed so healthy. "Chocolate chip cookies?" she asked meekly, trying to elicit permission to approach. She didn't want to offend the men by formally asking Billy if it was all right for her to pass out cookies. After all, she had been told by Warden DeJesus that all the men at Moriah Shock were

14

minimum security, non-violent felons, with short sentences, who were willing to work hard for early release.

Heidi had told her the majority of the inmates were drug users and dealers from the city, mostly marijuana and cocaine. Well marijuana, anyway, was as common as whiskey up here. Friends grew it and school teachers smoked it.

Billy stepped closer and smiled uneasily, keeping the thumb of one hand tucked under his belt. "Hey Chantal, aren't you the brave girl?"

"Well, Billy, you want me to just leave the basket?" She gave him one quick penetrating look with her blue eyes, that sent a wonderful time-delayed tingle down to his pelvis.

"Where d'ya get the boots, Chantal," he asked, stretching out the pronunciation of her name.

"When Heidi took us to Santa Fe," she paused, "trying to get a gallery for her paintings."

"Did she?" Billy asked.

Then Randy boldly asked, "Hey Miss, are the cookies for us?"

"Yes." She hesitated, not wanting to trespass on Billy's authority. "Yes, Billy, she did land a gallery. They all said they liked her foxes and her nudes."

Billy rolled his eyes at her choice of words. "Sure go ahead," Billy said to her, giving in to the situation. Turning to the inmates, he said, "One at a time. Line up, and Miss Beauvais here, will give you each a couple of cookies."

The men were surprisingly orderly, knowing Billy was breaking prison rules, allowing them unauthorized contact with an outsider, and a woman to boot. It was as if they wanted to show they weren't animals. Each one took a cookie from the basket. She smiled tenderly, feeling she was doing something good. Giovanni and Esteban simply nodded, bowed their heads slightly, said thank you, and lingered as long as they dared. By the time Randy waltzed up, he was emboldened, and started discussing the fine weather and this past winter's snowfall. And then Chico asked her how long she had lived here.

They were all so gentlemanly and smooth. Damian wasn't surprised. He knew brothers. They could be smooth like melted creamy butter and honey spread together on a morning muffin. Brothers could talk.

Damian decided to be last, right after Klocks who, under his passive exterior, was steaming mad. Billy was not exactly vigilant. He was busy staring at Chantal's profile as she handed out the cookies, following the dainty gold chain around her neck descending down in the shaded valley beneath her blouse.

Klocks and Randy were the only two white inmates on the work detail. Klocks didn't like black and Latino men overdoing it with white women. But he saw the situation. The white woman was out of line. She was encouraging them. Klocks moved up and seized a cookie, glaring at her. "You shouldn't be here, It's wrong. What you're doing to them is wrong."

Chantal froze and said nothing. Her eyes opened wide.

Damian witnessed it all. Now the feminine spell was broken; the mood was spoiled; the dream was tarnished, thanks to that honkie. Damian was crestfallen at seeing this spring flower wilt and get all nervous and worried, and her thinking she had done wrong, which she hadn't.

When Klocks turned away from her, crumbling his cookie in his tightening fist, Damian hissed into his ear. "You ass. You ruin everything."

Klocks just kept walking, scattering the crumbs from the crunched cookie. The other inmates, who were savoring their cookies, nibbling at them the way this Indian princess might have, saw what Klocks did, and took it as an insult to the lady.

Damian picked out his cookie, and Chantal gave a weak mechanical smile, feeling sorry she had ever walked over, wanting to get the hell out of there. Damian's chance to be as smooth as butter was gone, extinguished by Klocks.

Damian said lamely, "You're beautiful."

Billy was behind him, ready to escort Chantal away. Once he heard that, he said, "Hold it there, Damian. That's enough."

But Damian had one last thing to say to that bastard, that destroyer of life-giving moments, "And who's them, Klocks, who's them?"

Klocks was ready. He may have even orchestrated the whole thing, knowing how a young buck like Damian might react. Klocks whirled and shot out a roundhouse kick that caught Damian square in the side of the face and knocked him down. Like he had been hit by shovel.

The 21 Mine

Billy held up his club, but was immobilized by his concern for Chantal. In a voice she hadn't heard before, Billy shouted, "Chantal, get out of here!"

Klocks stood glowering over Damian. "Them is you, scumbag."

In an instant, the blacks in the crew pummeled Klocks down to the ground.

Billy stepped back from the melee and yelled "Eyeballs!" Trying to think, he looked around.

Chantal was running back to the main house, her back to everything. No one else was in sight.

"Fall in! Get off him! You won't graduate!" he yelled. 'You won't graduate,' sounded silly, but it worked. Freedom was why they were here. All the prisoners backed off. For most of them graduation was close, within two months, otherwise they might have continued taking out their resentment on Klocks, who, though bruised, smiled up at the blacks circled around him. Randy pushed through and pulled Klocks up off the soggy field.

Billy realized he was in deep shit. He should have known better than to let that fox stroll out here. He should have known it would mean trouble. Did he report this incident or not? The best he could do was to slant it his way. He hadn't asked Chantal to saunter out here in a dress and boots looking like she's ready for the cowgirls' version of the Rockettes.

Damian was still down and dazed. He didn't know of Klocks' black belt reputation. There was a lot he didn't know about Klocks. Actually, both their reputations were enhanced, Klocks as a mean and cold honkie and Damian as an idealistic black dude who had the guts to tell him off. That fight was how Klocks and Damian first met, on the last day of April, 1999. Little did they know that one day they would be bonded together in the prison lore of Upstate.

Jeff Kelly

three

Since his fight with Damian, Klocks was sequestered in a smaller, medium-security block surrounded by razor wire, sensors and surveillance cameras. The two-story, square brick building of four cells was reserved for incorrigible prisoners who couldn't handle the work and discipline of shock incarceration.

"Klocks!" the correction officer barked. "Front and center."

The C.O. yelled this command a dozen times a day to a dozen different inmates, but he was extra careful around Mr. Wallace Klocks. The C.O. harassed him, but didn't go overboard. He had read Klocks' file and read between the lines. He was the only prisoner who had been assigned from the Detective Syndicate rather than through the standard sentencing of the courts. The Syndicate had specified that Klocks be permitted to go out on work crews as long as he cooperated.

Nowhere was it stated, but if an inmate's file was marked D.S., it meant he had pled to a lesser offense in return for information given or promised in an ongoing investigation. In other words, he had turned state's evidence and was being paid to be an informer, a snitch.

Maybe Klocks was headed for the witness protection program. The guards didn't know for sure, but they knew enough not to fool with a D.S. inmate. Occasionally, guys sentenced by the D.S. were engaged in state-sanctioned, freelance, investigative reporting on the guards rather than the inmates.

"Warden A.D. wants to see you, Klocks," the C.O.said.

"Right," Klocks said dutifully. "Why?"

The C.O. disregarded the response. "Move out." Though he was nearly a foot taller than Klocks, the C.O. kept his distance, aware of Klocks' hobbies.

As he walked, Klocks was scanning his options. What advantage was there to be gained inside the Warden's office?

The C.O. escorted Mr. Wallace Klocks into Warden Adiaz DeJesus's plush office. "Remain here with Wallace. Thank you, John," Warden A.D. said to the C.O.

A.D. was the second Warden in the ten year history of Moriah Shock, and he was pleased to be here at a minimum facility with more of a boot camp, military atmosphere, than that of a prison. He tilted back in his swivel chair, balancing on two legs, looking and feeling dapper in his black, three-piece suit, studded diamond ring, and gold bracelet, legs apart. The impression he gave was one of cockiness born from experience. Unlike those who tried to disguise or temper their origins, especially if different from mainstream America, DeJesus relished his Puerto Rican heritage.

An example to others, especially Hispanics - that's how he viewed himself. He wore his black hair a tad longer than convention, so he could slick it straight back, the errant gray hair curling up. At age fifty-five, looking at retirement on a ninety thousand dollar a year pension, he was someone who had made it.

Whether he addressed an inmate or an outsider, the first lines of his speech were always the same. "My name is Warden Adiaz DeJesus," pronouncing each syllable of his name loudly and slowly. "I was born in the barrio of San Juan, Puerto Rico. When I was ten, my family and I moved to a Brooklyn ghetto. Now, forty-five years later, I am the highest ranking Spanish-speaking official in the New York State Correctional System. This is America. God bless America," and then in Spanish, "God bless Puerto Rico." And then again in English, "God bless the United States of America!" On the last syllable, the 'ca' in America, he would bang his fist on his desk, as if he were speaking from a podium. By that time, especially if this were the first time a visitor had met DeJesus, they were either saying 'Yes sir!' or sitting upright in stunned silence.

The 21 Mine

Klocks was different, a seasoned pro. Wardens had confronted him before, and he stood in front of A.D. unmoved. Besides he was busy carrying on his own research.

At all times, Klocks was gathering and storing data. Playing the admiring guest. He examined the photographs on the wall: A.D. talking to the governor, A.D. at the ground breaking ceremony for the renovations, and an aerial view of the buildings and grounds. Klocks was struck by the preponderance of forest and hills in all directions surrounding the prison. The hamlet of Mineville appeared as a tiny cluster of rooftops. The rest was the green forest of the Adirondacks with one large exception.

"What's that, a crater?" Klocks asked.

The Warden was a bit taken aback by Klocks' composure but A.D. had studied the history of the iron ore mines and liked to pontificate. "That, Wallace," began A.D. as he sauntered over to the framed photograph, "was the largest open pit mine in the country. In the early 1900's, the mines around here provided twenty-five percent of all the iron for this great country."

Klocks feigned disinterest while riveted to the picture and listening to the Warden's every word.

"Am I boring you? You know this is not why I called you here."

"I know," Klocks said in a monotone. "What else do you know about the mines, sir?"

"Tell me, Wallace, how deep would you guess those mines go?" Klocks was studying the photograph, memorizing as much as he could. "I have no idea, sir."

"Sit down and take a guess."

Klocks understood the Warden wanted a response, so he shrugged his shoulders, and said, "two hundred feet."

"Wallace, the 21 pit alone is more than four hundred feet deep and one thousand feet wide. Of the three shafts at the bottom of the pit, the deepest goes down eight thousand feet, ending one mile beneath the level of Lake Champlain. It took the miners in cages an hour and a half to get down there."

"That's impressive, sir." Klocks was staring at the aerial photograph, honing in on the pit. He was absorbing the details but dared not ask any more questions lest the Warden get suspicious.

Warden A.D. sat and held a piece of paper in front of him. He tapped his silver Mark Cross pen on his polished desk, until he was sure he had Wallace's full attention.

"Wallace, your recent behavior is troublesome and unacceptable. You're scheduled to appear in Albany Federal Court, Monday, May 17th, two weeks from today at 4:00 p.m. Federal marshals will be here at 10:00 a.m. to escort you. They're taking all precautions, Wallace. Three vehicles will be here."

Time to pay the fiddler, Klocks thought. The Warden studied Klocks for any reaction, but he automatically masked his feelings. 'Never let the enemy know what you're thinking,' was one of his mottoes.

"Why?" Klocks asked.

"Why?" the Warden repeated. "Surely, Wallace, you're the one who knows why. Apparently, you're an important witness, crucial to conviction in a very large smuggling case." The Warden waited patiently, before adding, "The Chinese Mafia?"

Klocks fidgeted in his chair.

The Warden observed one bead of sweat slide down Klocks' temple. That was unusual. Klocks was known as a cool customer, always poised and hardened. The Warden surmised that this must bother him.

"Your release remains scheduled for June 1st," A.D. stated. "Over my objections, " he added.

Klocks didn't smile. Most inmates, about to be released, were delightfully eager. Klocks seemed nonplused about it, almost unhappy.

The Warden was curious. A federal smuggling case was out of the ordinary. Plus, Klocks was uneasy. There was always a question of jurisdiction and security when transporting a prisoner - the only time correction officers carried weapons. The Warden was well aware that in a prior incident, Vermont officers had assumed New York officers had frisked and x-rayed Klocks. As Klocks entered the Vermont Court House, he set off a metal detector. Three sergeants held him down and with tweezers picked a key out of his nose. That key would have unlocked his handcuffs.

A.D. felt confident that with Klocks set to be released in one month an escape attempt would be foolhardy. Just to make sure that Klocks understood his concern, the Warden gave a final warning. "Any attempt to escape during transportation to or from your federal court date, and I will do my utmost to make sure you receive the harshest penalty available under the law."

Klocks had been taking a picture, developing and tracing it in his mind. He felt he could draw a fairly good copy of the aerial photograph of the 21 Mine. He preoccupied himself with this stratagem that only someone with a photographic memory could play.

He was disturbed to hear that he had to appear in court, and internally he was fighting to keep calm. He tried not to dwell on the news that he was to travel to federal court and testify against the largest smuggling kingpin in Chinatown, a warlord who was responsible for the illegal entry of thousands of Fukienese Chinese across the Canadian border into New York State. Maybe Klocks hadn't made such a smart bargain. The D.I. escorted him back to the brick house cell block where all Klocks did besides sit-ups and weighing his future options, was to lay down and think about his past.

* * * *

Wallace Klocks had been arrested and convicted several times on felony charges. In age, inner resolve, and criminal experience, Klocks was a man among boys. Warden Adiaz DeJesus had disapproved of the deal that brought him to Moriah Shock, and it was one of the few times the Warden was overruled. Among the inmates, Klocks was known as a street-wise career criminal with a genuine knowledge of art and antiques whose specialty was outwitting the law and his companions in crime.

Klocks had convinced himself that he had a special sixth sense. At its most elementary, the sense was akin to a photographic memory. At its most sophisticated, it was a prescient sense of where and when things were going to happen, and an ability to influence others. He called it his ability to transcend.

Jeff Kelly

When delving in memory, he relaxed his mind, tried to keep it empty and open, waiting for something to be revealed. Klocks felt most people tried too hard to remember things. He had the confidence to let the information surface. Wait, stay calm, and if at any time in the past his mind had been exposed to a particular piece of data, his mind would find it - as long as he wasn't bombarding the synapses with confusing demands.

Klocks had mastered the calmness and confidence necessary for recalling names, places and pictures, and had moved beyond to a form of mental telepathy. Klocks had persuaded himself that at certain times he had a gift for sensing what people were thinking, and then visualizing and even swaying or bending their actions. After he used this ability to transcend to his advantage, he would glowingly refer to it as "My Gift."

four

The dinner whistle sounded and Klocks twitched back to the present.
The brick house guard escorted him down the cast iron stairwell.
Klocks stood at attention and waited for his platoon to come marching by,
chanting "left, left, left, right, left." The drill instructor bellowed out "march and
halt." Klocks fell in at the end of the column. Tonight was Monday, when they
were fed something else besides potatoes and liverwurst stew. Klocks' platoon
marched into the cafeteria with Randy carrying their colors, executing a crisp
right hand turn at the worn spot in the tile floor, squaring the corner, trying not to
get yelled at. Randy proceeded to insert the platoon flag with the newly earned
streamers in the stand up front.

Klocks sniffed the air. Randy fell in line behind him. "It's Chinese. I heard
it was good. Packed with cockroaches," Randy said without moving his lips.

"Are you talking?" barked the D. I. "Give me fifty. I want fifty." Randy
was only 140 pounds, all wiry, and loved doing push-ups. His one goal was to be
totally exhausted by the end of the day, so he could sleep through the night,
instead of thinking about how he had totally screwed up. Klocks, on the other
hand, regularly slept like a baby, and felt that he had done all right, except for
the killings, which no one, but one detective, even suspected.

Randy popped up, out of breath. "Sir. Yes sir!" He fell back in line, hungry
for Chinese.

Jeff Kelly

The chefs were drawn from the inmate population, and each chef prided himself on two or three ethnic entries from his homeland. Out of a prison population of about two hundred and ninety, five or six were Asian. One Chinese was known as Funny Fungi because he was always laughing. Fungi was dishing out the main course and making sure each prisoner got a fortune cookie.

When Fungi caught sight of Klocks coming with his tray, he fumbled under his smock for a particular fortune cookie. "This fortune cookie for you, Mr. Klocks." Fungi knew he was taking his chances, with Klocks, and with the system. Fungi was a short-timer, due to be released with the next class. But he had his own orders.

Klocks eyed Fungi warily. Fungi had never said a word to him. "This is real fortune-telling cookie," Fungi said in a high, nasal voice ending in a toothy grin. Klocks left the cookie on his tray where Fungi had put it and executed the required two steps to the side and two back. "Column move. Let's go, move. Ready seats. Table six. Sit!"

Eight men sat, gobbling their rice bowls of chicken lo mein, well-seasoned with Teriyaki sauce. All but Klocks, who with one hand cracked open his fortune cookie. On one side of the tiny strip of white paper was the standard, "You will grow happy and prosperous." Klocks shrugged and was about to show bad manners and eat the shell, when he turned the paper over. On the other side, scrawled in red ink, next to a drawing of a rat with chopsticks sticking out of its eyes, were the words, "Testify and die."

Klocks slowly raised his head and looked up front to the kitchen. As the serving line of the next platoon parted, Klocks caught the laughing eyes of the black-haired Fungi staring at him.

Randy took his first breather from shoveling in food, and glanced at Klocks, whose furrowed forehead on a usually impassive face caught Randy's attention. Randy thought Klocks was disappointed with a bland fortune. "They don't take chances with these fortune cookies anymore," he said. "Right, Klocks?"

Klocks emptied his rice bowl onto Randy's plate while he crumbled the cookie in his clenched hand, stood, and approached the drill instructor. "Seconds, sir?"

The 21 Mine

Boldly, in the proper military style, Klocks strode to the back of the line of the next platoon. Fungi was watching him, and his mind raced.

Fungi laughed aloud nervously as he saw danger coming toward in the form of Klocks, who displayed his own inscrutable look of contentment and pointed to the tray of rice. Using a wooden spoon, Fungi stopped laughing, and keeping his eyes on Klocks, dished out another gooey bowl of rice. He tapped the bowl and murmured, "I am only the messenger." Fungi was relieved to see that the drill instructor, Spike, whom they all called Hurricane, was standing directly behind Klocks.

"I am only a man," responded Klocks, taking two steps to the side as if to move on.

Fungi thought Klocks had said his piece.

Klocks took one step backward as if to take another and turn and leave, but instead pivoted off his back foot, tossing his tray over his shoulder, and sprung up waist high, twisting in mid-air, unwinding a roundhouse kick at the head of Fungi. "And here's your fortune," grunted Klocks as he slammed his heel into the Adam's apple of Fungi, whose wooden spoon went twirling high in the air.

Klocks' sense of coordination was on high alert. He knew his mission and didn't hesitate. He moved fast and the spoon moved slowly, as if it were falling in slow motion. As Klocks landed sideways, bending the aluminum tray bars, he caught the spoon in his right hand, instinctively slammed his elbow backwards into the gut of Hurricane, whom he actually liked, and with the extra second he had bought, choked up on the spoon handle and stabbed at Fungi's head as it sagged onto the serving counter. Klocks was aiming for an eye, but succeeded in hitting an ear, the spoon sticking out as the Chinaman slid off the counter, unconscious, blood dripping onto the spoon.

Klocks braced himself for a beating as Hurricane and the other guards hammered him to the floor with blows to his body. Hurricane locked him in a suffocating choke hold. Klocks had broken the rules; he expected and deserved this. He didn't resist, except to protect himself.

"You're finished, here, Klocks! You're out of here!" Hurricane yelled through clenched teeth. The place erupted in the howls of a professional wrestling match. The guards dragged Klocks by his feet, but he had made his point. You mess with me, I mess with you. If he had done nothing, forget it; no one would have respected him.

The guards dragged him out of the cafeteria across the sidewalk over the pavement, bumping his head on the curb on the way to the brick house. Hurricane stood him up, pushed him up the iron stairs of the old mine shop, and tossed him back into his cell, the clothes ripped off his back. Klocks closed his eyes and felt his face and the back of his head. Not bad, two bruises. He coughed and grimaced from the pain of a cracked rib on his left side. The muscles around his hip were strained from where the energy and torque had flowed down to his foot, until he hit his mark, just as he was taught.

Wallace rolled onto his bed and closed his eyes to collect himself. Usually, a prisoner with two fights in a week would be shipped out immediately, but the Warden's policy was thrown asunder by the federal decree requiring Klocks to testify. The federal thing was mucking up the works all the way around. Klocks figured he was doomed. If he did testify, the Chinese would catch up with him, unless he was placed in the witness protection program, or unless he put himself in his own witness protection program; his own stab at anonymity.

The first option was out. He had refused the official federal program, because he realized that his life of gainful thievery, of free choice, would be forever over. He'd get fat and bored. Imagine staying within sight of federal agents somewhere in a faceless suburb, twenty-four hours a day for the next twenty years, drinking beer and watching TV. Intolerable. He'd rather be dead, he really would.

Within hours, if not minutes, everyone in Moriah Shock had heard the news about Klocks attacking Fungi. But few, including Damian, had any idea why. The attack cemented Klocks' reputation as an unpredictable solo artist.

Even the guard Billy couldn't help but be curious. Billy's one weakness was his love of his fellow man. He was like a tipsy Irishman soaking up the sounds of gibberish at the pub, convinced that he's partaking of the pungent conversation of poet laureates. He wanted to hear Klocks' version and received permission from the brick house guard to stop by.

"Klocks, I don't know why you're still here, but I'm watching you," Billy said.

The 21 Mine

"Sir, if you were in my shoes, you would have done what I done. The damn Chinese want to kill me."

Klocks had a conversation with Billy that helped him clear up his own thinking, an unseen process that most convicts avoided. Klocks looked at the big picture and he liked to call his own shots. The Chinese fortune cookie confirmed what his intuition had already told him. If he went to Albany to testify, as he had agreed and signed, he was walking a tightrope from which he was sure to topple. The next time he went to order Chinese in Troy, one of Fu Chow's druggies would puncture his lung with an ice pick.

Turn state's evidence and die, that's what will happen. On the other hand, if he didn't testify, he'd be transferred back to the maximum hell of Dannemora to serve out his sentence.

After Billy left, Klocks needed to get away. Away from a prison cell in the Adirondacks. He closed his eyes and drifted back to the same place he was when the dinner whistle sounded - to when he was a boy in Troy in the summer. He used to swim underwater, come up behind the Poestenkill waterfall and climb the slippery rocks and find dry ledges and small undercut caves. Klocks liked caves. When he was mad at his Mom, he'd hide there for hours. The pounding noise drowned out any other sounds, and depending on the volume of water and the spray and mist, he could go to sleep lying on a high ledge tucked back in against the cool rock, and not think about the noise of the bed creaking when his mom came home with another man.

Those thoughts didn't bother him now, but they did then. Every time a different man came home, Klocks retaliated by honing his skills, by breaking into pawn shops and antique stores. And when his mom asked where he got the old radio, or the gold pocket watch, he'd say "your boyfriend gave it to me. the one you were with last night." And she wouldn't say anything. Soon his room was filled with valuable items, like he was a real collector. In fact, he'd brag to his friends while playing stick ball in the streets. "I'm a collector," he would say. He loved the sound of the word 'collector', but his friends didn't have a clue, except that as time passed none of their moms would let them play with him. "The boy is a professional thief," one mom said.

Jeff Kelly

He didn't go after CD players or new digital watches. He liked the old, the antique. He felt there was no art in taking what's new. Might as well just steal money. Besides, if you stole a TV, you had to deal with serial numbers. Have you ever seen an antique Windsor chair with a serial number? Who's to say who owns a Winslow Homer drawing? The person who had it probably bought it from someone who stole it. How is someone going to say which Audubon print is theirs? Klocks always changed the number anyway. He felt that a print belonged to the original artist, to John Audubon, and to a dandy like himself who knew the value of it, knew a New York City folk art dealer who could list it in a Sotheby's auction as legit. In his own eyes, he wasn't a thief. He was an antique dealer.

five

Early the next morning, Klocks witnessed a squirrel get zapped by an electrified trip wire which encircled the brick house cells. I got to find me that squirrel, Klocks thoughts. Maybe Randy could snatch me some road kill. I got to find me a dead squirrel. Klocks went back into control mode. He felt kind of special being the only inmate in a cell with bars in all of Moriah Shock.

In the evening, after dinner, within view of a C.O., he was permitted to fraternize for half an hour with his platoon. He collected peanut butter, paid with money and cigarettes, and no one thought twice about it, figuring he wanted the peanut butter because he was planning on doing some queer in the shower. Klocks didn't care what anyone thought. Water and peanut butter, that's all Klocks needed to live on. Up to now, his philosophy of 'one man *is* an island' had always been his strength.

Klocks concluded that a lot of prisoners preferred life in minimum to life on the streets. The sleep was regular, the food was better, and the exercise was forced. Prisoners were healthier, mentally and physically, than when they were back in the ghetto.

That was the core problem the early release programs confronted. The prisoners gained by signing up for this boot-camp like environment. They gained discipline, esprit de corps and a work ethic. And then they got out early - that was all good. But, when they rode the bus directly back to their neighborhoods, the same cycles of despair and defeat eventually sucked them in, until three and

31

four years down the road, the reformed prisoners committed the same crimes all over again, and ended up growing old back Upstate.

Not to die though. No one wanted to die in the slammer, and let their sons and daughters, wives and girlfriends, bear the cross of knowing their father, or their man, had died in prison. In that one way, Klocks was like any other prisoner. He didn't want to die in prison. He especially didn't want to die anonymously in prison. Dying in prison was a primordial fear of all prisoners, and the older ones panicked at a cough, thinking they were about to die. Klocks wanted the front page. Dying while trying to escape. That was okay.

Klocks was in a bind. He had to get out. But because of his fights with Damian and Fungi, he was now incarcerated in a locked cell, fulfilling the erroneous image of bars and keys that most Adirondackers had of Moriah Shock. Klocks figured that whatever he did, he had to make it look haphazard. After all, what sane man would try to escape from prison when he was going to be released in one month? Klocks needed a new identity. He needed to go back to the womb and be born again. He needed to be reincarnated.

He walked down the corridor to the bathroom, still within the bars of the brick cell block. The bathroom had no windows, only a twelve inch exhaust fan. With his thumb, Klocks nudged out some dry mortar from a corner, which crumbled in his hands. An exposed pipe wrapped in insulation ran underneath the cracked ceiling. Maybe it was an asbestos pipe. Sitting on the can, he decided then and there to do what Klocks did best, to take action. He would go on a fast protesting the deteriorating conditions of the jail.

The only solids he would eat would be the peanut butter he had hoarded. When he wrestled in high school at 121 pounds, he used to drop five pounds in the two days before the weigh-in. He'd skip lunch, dinner and the next morning's breakfast. If he were still over the limit, he'd put on the plastic sweat suit, and do jumping jacks in the sauna room. An assistant coach watched in case he fainted. After he made weight, he was allowed a three pound recovery and ate a healthy lunch of salad and spaghetti.

Klocks was like an Arab, the way he could eat a big meal and store it in his system, or like an Arab's camel, the way he could store water. In the days ahead, he would have to push his knack for survival to a greater extent than even he had imagined.

After the first day of refusing meals, Warden A. D. was apprised of Klocks' tactic. He notified the guards to watch Klocks closely and make sure the press didn't find out. He told Billy and Hurricane to tell the other guards, "If there's a leak, it's your job." The guards had a union, but a warden could make a guard's life miserable by dishing out bad assignments, like working Christmas and New Year's Eve.

For three days Klocks fasted, drinking water and the prison's version of kool-aid. He was losing weight, shrinking himself, making himself smaller. Each time he went to the bathroom, he squeezed out all the piss and shit he could from his scrawny body, and then stood on the toilet seat and used a dime with a flattened edge to unscrew one of the four screws in the fan unit, replacing the screw so it just barely held in the fan.

The last time Klocks went to the can, he kept only his underwear on, stuffing his clothes in his Nike bag, along with a candle, flashlight and jars of peanut butter. He stood on the toilet seat, removed the fan cover, chinned himself on the edge of the opening, and like a snake, squeezed into the square hole, one arm, a shoulder, then his head. He knew if he could get his head through, he could make it. Unlike most prisoners, he had actually thought about what to do if he got out.

Incredibly, he was fully wedged into a ten inch by ten inch vent. It was night, so the six foot long vent was black, but he could see the greenish glimmer of a parking lot light through the inside of the louvered vent opening high up on the outside west wall of the jail.

The onset of claustrophobia was a problem. Once in the shaft he needed to keep moving. His breathing was constricted. He could only inch forward when he exhaled. He was afraid of getting stuck and suffocating from not being able to expand his lungs. He was afraid he might wheeze for help. Most of all, he was perplexed and troubled by his own thoughts of panic.

The outside wall was three stories of brick, all varying colors, the older ones light orange, the newer ones, filling in where windows used to be, dark red. Two decorative rows of bricks, eight feet apart were set out ever so slightly, probably an attempt to give the wall some texture. When the building was built about 1910, the Witherbee Sherman masons must have gotten bored with their repetitive rows of bricks, and as they progressed higher, threw in two innovative rows which protruded two inches from the rest of the brick wall.

As Klocks wormed closer to the louvered opening on the wall, his feet were still sticking out in the space above the bathroom stall. He had removed the shoelaces from his prison-issued Riddell boots and stuffed one shoelace and his running shoes in the Nike bag he was dragging behind, attached to his ankles by the other shoelace. He could feel the bag catch on the casing for the fan above the toilet seat. If he yanked abruptly, he'd be free, but he might break the laces and lose his survival bag.

If his escape attempt failed, he wanted his bag back. Inside, were New Balance running shoes, which had been mailed to him a week ago. The trendy running shoes were one of his few possessions, and he had good use for them. He paused for a moment before he tried to work the bag up over the brick and mortar, trying to recall if he had put the seat down, lest his new sneakers plop into the toilet.

Undulating his hips and stomach like a reptile, exhaling, he managed to inch back until his ankles showed up again near the ceiling inside the bathroom. With the toes of one foot he worked the knot around to the back of his other ankle. He wiggled forward again until the bag bumped and caught on the lip. As he held his ankles up against the top of the tin casing of the shaft, he performed a painful twirling motion as if he were screwing himself into the shaft, grunted, and the bag thumped safely into the shaft.

From head to the dragging bag, he was firmly stuffed and stretched into the shaft. The tin was thin and malleable, and the shaft was so tight that it crinkled and groaned, molding to his body and head as he squirmed forward. Bits of dried mortar and twigs were stamped into his forehead and face. He worried that if he became trapped, the tin shaft might become his coffin. This happened to a city friend in the 1970's, who, desperate to gain admittance to Studio 54, crawled in through a shaft in the dance floor ceiling, got stuck there and died.

Klocks was disturbed with himself for allowing thoughts of death to enter his mind at a time like this, when death was entirely plausible. He firmly believed that whatever he focused on would manifest itself. His prescient sense worked on own subconscious too. If he thought about dying, it might come to pass.

With his outstretched arm and hand leading this six feet journey, he flipped aside a pile of twigs and dried mud from some nesting swallows and pushed on the louver at the other end. Through repetitive twisting and poking with his forefinger, where the slats were rotten, he was able to open a fist size hole to the outside. He could neither move his head to see what he was doing nor fully expand his lungs. He spent the next hour taking short, quick breaths as he gouged out most of the wood with his bloody fingers, enlarging the jagged hole in the louvers until he had progressed to picking away at the wooden frame.

Finally, he pulled and twisted himself closer and with his head butted the crumbling slats, punctured the barrier, and gulped the night air. He was surprised at how high he was, and swiveled his head around looking for a pipe or something to grab onto. He was too far from either corner of the building. Momentarily stymied, he watched a guard in the far parking lot flick pine needles off his new Dodge Ram. Klocks felt neither animosity nor envy toward the guard. Just felt he had nothing in common with what looked like the normal behavior of a middle class citizen and his prized possession. The only thing Klocks felt was relief when the guard drove his pick-up away.

He poked out his chest and his other arm from the brick wall, looking as if he were about to do a swan dive, but the height was too much. He studied the wall below and fixated on a row of bricks with the corners angled outward. If he could get his big toe and the inside of the ball of his foot on that imperceptible ledge, maybe he could stand. But he needed something to cling to with his hands.

If a guard had looked up through the greenish street lighting outside the jail, he would have seen a man's body sticking out of a brick wall, bulging, as if it were a large snake leaving a small hole.

Craning his neck, Klocks saw that directly above him was another set of angled bricks. The bottom of that upper ledge might work, if he could reach. Two fingers pressing against the underside of those cantilevered bricks, and maybe, like a black cat, he could inch his way to the corner of the building. He was five eight and the vertical distance between the two sets of bricks looked to be about eight feet. With his arms stretched above him, he might be able to reach and hold himself against the wall while he worked his way to the corner of the building.

After two minutes of pressing against and between the two rows of cantilevered bricks, scraping his chest bloody, and sticking to the wall by friction, Klocks reached out with his left hand, relieving the shoulder of the stress from holding his arms high above him, and grabbed the corner of the building, finally feeling safe and secure, about how a normal person would feel when reaching a ladder from high on a roof. Klocks was sinewy, with no measurable body fat, and he simply clamped on the corner with his hands and feet and shinnied down like he was a monkey on his favorite vine.

In the dark dampness which Klocks didn't feel, he took slow breaths to relax. From around his waist, Klocks pulled out a long thin, nearly-invisible, fly-fishing filament. His back pressed against the brick wall, he was looking for the dead squirrel that the guards had tossed against the building - after it had been electrocuted by the high voltage.

Klocks spotted it lying on the drainage stone in the corner. From the bottom of his bag he removed some folded pieces of cardboard which he wrapped around his arms and legs, tying them on with pieces of shoelace. After he applied the makeshift armor, he kicked the dead carcass and picked the squirrel up by its rigid tail. He wound three loops of the filament around the squirrel's neck and tied a loose slip knot. Using an underhand toss, he flung the squirrel onto the lighted section of the electric fence, saw the sparks, and waited for the alarm. As the alarm sounded, he jiggled the line to make the frenzied squirrel look like it was making its last spasmodic movements, and then released the slip knot and reeled in. He quickly put on the leather gloves.

The guard on duty monitored the last working surveillance camera and then looked out the window. Just as he suspected, another damn squirrel had fried itself on twelve thousand volts of electricity. Turning off the alarm, he switched off the voltage and the underground sensors, and grabbed his flashlight. The guard, Hurricane, was annoyed, because he had told his girlfriend he'd call her around 8:00 p.m. and it was almost 8:00. He picked up the phone and checked in with the D.I. on duty. "Mike, yeah, another damn squirrel. I've shut the power off and I'm going out."

Klocks figured the power was off because his squirrel was no longer sparking. He pushed away from the brick wall, as casually as if he had been standing on the corner watching the girls go by, and walked over to a darkened section of the fourteen foot high fence, which was topped with rows of twelve inch razor wire, called Israeli wire. If Klocks touched the electrified wire with the palm of his hand, and it was live, the paralyzing voltage would close his hand around the wire. He squatted down and using the back of his gloved hand, touched the electrified wire down near the ground. No shock. Immediately, he scrambled over the three lines of current and then gingerly climbed the fence with the razor wire. He jumped and rolled. He left pieces of shredded cardboard, clinging to the wire. Better that than his skin. The blood of one thin cut warmed his wrist.

Thirty yards away, Hurricane was putting on his disposable gloves, as prescribed by universal precautions. He strode over to the first wire and grabbed the squirrel by the tail, flinging it in the darkened corner of the brick building the way he had done a few nights ago.

Later on, he claimed he had been aware of the hardness of the tail, thinking rigor mortis had set in awfully quickly. But at the time, it was a passing thought, lost in the moment. Once inside the guardhouse, he removed the latex gloves and dropped them in the trash barrel before he reached for the lever to turn on the power.

He keyed in the phone number for his girlfriend, but the line was busy. Who was talking to his girlfriend at 8:00 on a Friday night? Maybe her mother from Vermont. Until he got through to his girlfriend, he'd be fraught with jealousy and suspicion.

By that time, Klocks was racing across the spongy, brown grounds on his way to being anonymous, amorphous and eternal. The physical tension of the exertion had given him a mental Zen-like high, and he was exuding power from his heightened state, almost as if he had drained the voltage from the electric fence and absorbed it himself.

Jeff Kelly

six

The night of Klocks' escape was the same day million dollar renovations on the prison were finally completed. On the boundary line of Moriah Shock Incarceration, not far from Heidi Beauvais's ranch, officials had dedicated a blue and gold New York State historical sign. The cast bronze tablet commemorated the Fisher Hill Mine, like a tombstone burying the last wisps of grief for a dead iron ore industry. Heidi had spearheaded the group that insisted there be some sort of plaque.

The first Warden, A.D.'s predecessor, had referred to Heidi and her daughters as "a bunch of gypsies," which piqued A.D.'s interest. From the start, ten years ago, she had opposed the transformation of the abandoned mine into a prison. Right after the ceremony, on Friday afternoon, Warden Adiaz DeJesus finally paid Heidi a long-promised visit.

She was Moriah Shock's closest neighbor. Heidi still stubbornly referred to the prison as 'the mine' after the original Fisher Hill Mine. When she opened her plain wooden front door, Heidi stood tall, a jumble of silver bracelets reflecting the light, her ponytails hanging straight down her chest, accentuating her firm posture and adopted Indian heritage. She led A.D. to a red, cushioned armchair and graciously offered him a blue bottle of sparkling Saratoga water. As he settled into the comfortable armchair sipping the carbonated water, he took in the cozy, cabin-like surroundings. This is the way to conduct business, he thought.

Heidi had locked the malamutes in the back pen and shooed away her tiger cat, who had hissed at the Warden. "Tell me more about Attica," Heidi said diplomatically. "You touched on that experience when you gave your speech."

A.D. sat spellbound, staring at one of Heidi's paintings. He put down the water. "All right." He loosened his tie. "When you start out as a C.O., you're placed in the worse maximum security prisons, like Dannemora and Comstock here Upstate, and of course Sing Sing and Attica. And I had one of the worse shifts, 4:00 to midnight. In this case, that may have saved my life. When the Attica prisoners rioted and took over D wing, I wasn't there. The riot started about 11:00 in the morning, and by 2:00 in the afternoon the inmates controlled all of D block and had taken hostages." He paused to take another sip.

"Well, Ms. Beauvais," A.D. continued.

Heidi interrupted. "It's Miss Beauvais. Heidi is fine."

Outwardly, Warden A.D. didn't blink. Inwardly, he was quite pleased at her honest admission, since he had heard that she was divorced from a younger man from nearby Westport.

"Well, Heidi, when I showed up for my shift at 4:00 p.m., I was the only guard around who spoke Spanish. So the state needed a translator and I was officially asked. Drafted. I was nervous. I would have to go in with no weapon, and we were hearing ghastly reports of makeshift weapons and two guns that had fallen into the hands of the inmates.

"Governor Rockerfeller was addressing me, twenty-seven years old, on the speaker phone in the Warden's paneled office. The white-haired men standing around wished me good luck as if I might not return. I had my instructions. I read from the Bible before I went in. I carried a tape recorder with me, but when the inmates frisked me they confiscated that. The prisoners even took my shoelaces. I guess they learned from us. Should I stop, Heidi? It's all history. "

"No Warden, I'm. . ."

"Please call me Adiaz, or A.D. if you prefer. The guards all call me Warden A.D."

"When I walked in, alone and naked but for pants, pencil and paper, I remembered one thing from my Bible readings. God is love. God is truth. And if your mind is full of love and truth, there is no room for error. I filled my mind with love and committed myself to telling the truth.

"Some other day, I'll tell you the details of my three negotiating sessions, and the evil I saw from the inmates, and the evil from the state forces that retook the prison. I learned then that no one person, group or race has a monopoly on good or evil.

"The Latino inmates respected me and wrote notes to their mothers and girl friends that I promised to deliver. I like to think I saved a few lives on both sides, but I never knew until ten minutes after I walked out of my third session, that Rockerfeller had ordered the state police to retake the prison. I learned about force and justice."

He raised the blue bottle to his lips. "Apparently, the importance of a Spanish speaking officer was imbedded in the state officials, and from Attica onward I was rapidly promoted."

"Congratulations, A.D.," Heidi said. They both smiled pleasantly at her use of his nickname.

Heidi's three daughters were in town in Port Henry, and though Heidi and the Warden had communicated before about the plaque, and about the new construction which she had objected to, they had never sat down alone and spoken to each other personally. So they were a little uneasy.

Heidi got up and took a framed family photo off the mantle above the fireplace. What A.D. saw in the picture was an American Indian woman with a wrinkled face and grayish-black, braided hair at the head of a procession of three funky women, wearing colorful, calf-length flowered dresses, sweeping the air above cowboy boots.

A.D. handed her back the picture and said, "The regal matriarch of the unflinching Beauvais clan. You have an Indian mystique and your daughters are beautiful."

To Heidi's ears, he couldn't have said anything more perfect. "Thank you," she said, glowing with radiance, convinced of his eloquence.

He chose this moment to deliver his more formal message. He assured her that Moriah Shock was not being reclassified as medium security, which had been one of Heidi's fears when the expansion was announced. She and her daughters would continue to be safe in their ranch house so close to the prison.

Heidi responded frankly. "I'll admit it. This town's been hurting. We've needed the jobs. If it had to be a prison, then it's a prison. At least the Park Agency approved, and the leaf peepers can't complain."

"That's right, this is an environmentally-friendly, non-polluting industry."

"Yes A.D., but don't you think eighteen prisons in the Adirondacks is enough? Almost all built in the last twenty years."

A.D. said nothing.

"We live closer than anyone else to the Fisher Hill Mines," she paused to look around.

Anticipating her concern, A.D. reminded her. "Inmates don't want to escape from a minimum. To escape would be counterproductive. They're only here for six months, and if they make it, they're free."

Heidi couldn't quite see the prison from her picture window, but she certainly heard the construction. She appreciated his assurance. So far, she said, the only problem was her "dogs barking and the dishes rattling."

"Dishes rattling? You mean what, the bulldozers caused the dishes to vibrate?" asked the Warden, incredulous.

"I'm sorry. No it's the mines, not the prison."

"The mines," repeated A.D. "I've been studying the mines and I'm fascinated. I've taken a book out of the Port Henry Library called 'Through The Light Hole,' but I haven't finished it." Clapping his hands, leaning forward as he pushed aside the crackers, he asked Heidi, "Can you educate me?"

"I'll try. I can at least tell you why the dishes make noises. First, you have to understand, mining is finished here, but the mines aren't."

Heidi was starting to enjoy his company, and what had begun as strictly business was sliding into the social. She talked on as she got up to switch off the glaring kitchen light. "It's all honeycombed down there. They're always changing; filling with water, collapsing, rattling dishes here and in Witherbee." She stopped talking to sit back down, rocking back, holding her knees together and laughing with her dark eyes. All of which enthralled A.D.

The 21 Mine

"Years ago, my youngest daughter was afraid our house was haunted, until I explained about the maze of tunnels underneath us, filling up with water. Sarah Hayes, in the village, had to move her pastry business. Her house was shaking so from the shifting catacombs thousands of feet below, her cakes wouldn't rise."

Warden A.D. was mesmerized by her description and basked in the presence of this painter and rancher whose feather in her hair perpetuated her Indian image. Whether pretense or not, he didn't know, nor did he care. She was making an effort to be and do something special. Looking around at her parlor and all Heidi's paintings, A.D. said, "I'll need something, sort of a housewarming gift, to warm up my office. One of your paintings; maybe one of the foxes, might look grand."

"They're all for sale," she said. "The red fox is twelve hundred dollars. The fox crossing the frozen river is seventeen hundred dollars."

Warden A.D. spied a stuffed red fox in the corner, next to the wood box, and realized that it was probably her model, but discreetly said nothing.

"I'll see what my budget allows for," he commented.

"Here's an album of my recent work," Heidi said as she gestured in the direction of the stone fireplace and the one painting that had made A.D. straighten and take notice. Above the mantle, which was one solid slab of granite, was a large painting of a nude woman languishing, lying down in the lush outdoors, next to a tiger.

A.D. ventured into new territory and asked, "Who modeled for the woman?"

"One of my daughters."

Now that he had broken that barrier, he asked quickly, "Is it for sale? How much?"

"It's not for sale. But generally my nudes go for about three thousand dollars."

"You know, Heidi, there is an artist, an inmate, who is going to do an island scene, a mural on the cafeteria wall. I'd be interested to see what you think?"

He stepped closer to her. "I'd love to have one of your paintings of an Adirondack scene; maybe one of your foxes? Buying it outright might be a problem for me. But we could do a trade. I have work crews that go out into the woods. I see you don't have men around, perhaps we could do some work on the ranch, and in return, you could donate a painting to my office to give it that Adirondack, native touch."

When he needed to, A.D. could be creative and charming, captivated as he was by this woman fully his age, lined in the face, but steadfast; someone who had made a name for herself here in the abject poverty of rural Essex County.

Heidi wasn't attracted to him in any physical way, but she recognized he was the CEO of the biggest employer in town. "I might need work on the ranch; fence building, for some horses I plan to board. It would certainly be worth the painting of a fox."

A.D. hesitated, and picked up a horseshoe off the mantle. He thought more about what he was suggesting. "Since I know your land borders the prison's, we could probably get away with it."

The transaction was surely against state regulations. Certainly a little out of the ordinary for a warden. But favors were granted, and Warden Adiaz DeJesus ran the show and was well respected.

A.D. put the horseshoe back on the mantle and Heidi strolled to the door. A.D. turned and took a last look at the nude woman and the tiger, and thought privately that someday he would own that painting and possess the artist. He looked outside at the gray Cadillac where the driver, Billy, was absorbed in the Sports Illustrated swimsuit issue. Officially New York State wardens did not rate a limousine, but Billy didn't mind and didn't notify the union. He figured maybe he'd get a chance to talk up Heidi's daughter Chantal

Besides, A.D. had arranged for Billy to be transferred from Comstock to Moriah Shock, so Billy could be closer to his dad, who was the supervisor of Elizabethtown and was dying of cancer. The warden had done him a favor, and Billy owed him and knew when to keep his mouth shut. Anyway, Billy liked the Warden, because the Warden functioned without being brutal and he was curious about life in the cold Adirondack Mountains, Billy's favorite place.

"Thank you for stopping over," Heidi said standing and swaying, one arm crossed over her vest, the other extended to shake good-bye.

The 21 Mine

A.D. gently grabbed her hand, holding on rather than shaking. She was comfortable around men, and neither A.D.'s manner nor his city suit were intimidating her. He surprised himself and her, though she didn't show it, by gently pulling her toward him and kissing her on the cheek.

"Quite a woman," A.D. said as Billy opened the back door of the car for him.

"Watch your coat, sir."

When Billy started the limo, Heidi remained standing in the doorway. A.D. watched her, questioning his own timber, as Billy pulled a U-turn out of the driveway onto Lincoln Pond Road back to Moriah Shock. A.D. said quickly, "Honk your horn." But she had already stepped inside, and A.D. was left staring at the barn. I must see her again, he thought. Some evening. He was already staying four nights a week at the cottage next to the prison, but he was bored at night. He had no cable and lousy reception.

A.D. had glimpsed domestic, country life with Heidi, which left him with a feeling that maybe he had missed something along the way. "Billy, remind me to order a case of that Saratoga water, the blue bottles."

A.D. brushed off his coat, and reached down to wipe and polish one toe of his shoe with his suede glove. Warden A.D. was approaching retirement age, and he was where he wanted to be; in a minimum security prison doing his last few years, at $138,000 a year. Those last three years were the key ones for a healthy pension, enabling him to retire to his condo on the beautiful beaches of Mayaquez, one of the few Puerto Ricans to have conquered the States.

He had done his time Upstate, just like the prisoners, in maximum security, emotional hellholes like Dannemora and Comstock, where the average life span of a guard was a little less than that of a New York City cop - about 57 years, or more than ten years below the average white male.

In each prison he had commanded, he was a role model. To the Hispanic inmates; from the Dominican Republic, who were in the majority, from Colombia, from Haiti, and of course from Puerto Rico, Warden Adiaz DeJesus was a Latino who had made it. He always addressed them in Spanish and with respect. They loved him for that. And they envied him for the money he made and the way he looked, dapper and polished, wearing a suit and shiny black shoes inmates could see their reflection in. If they hadn't made it, at least he had, and they knew him. And when he walked the hallways and the yards, unarmed, his black hair slicked back, his belly sucked in, a diamond on his pinkie and a gold chain on his wrist all he heard was, "Hi Boss," "Good morning, sir," and from the blacks, with their heads slightly down, not wanting to draw too much attention to themselves, "All right, now. Yes sir."

A.D. outlined the fence building proposition to Billy. He sensed the Warden had his eye on Heidi, which explained why she was going to get her fences built for free by prison labor, something generally reserved for the municipalities. Billy pushed the lock button, and the simultaneous click of the four doors reminded them both of prison gates.

* * * *

In two minutes, Billy pulled in to the parking lot next to the Warden's Jeep. For a moment, A.D. stayed in the back of the limo on the car phone making sure all was well at the prison one hundred yards away. He knew if he walked into his office, he'd be there another hour. Something would come up. Instead, he hung up, thanked Billy, grabbed his black briefcase, unlocked his jeep and drove away. It was Friday night.

On the way up on Monday, he had cut west off the Northway at Exit 29 in North Hudson and had seen only one car in the twenty, serpentine miles through the mountain marshes and trailheads. Darkness and his aversion to risk made for an easy decision. He drove down the hill, taking a right at the Chinese restaurant onto Port Henry's Main Street and Route 22 south toward Ticonderoga, where he spotted his first McDonald's and felt more at home.

During the first part of his two hour drive back down toward Albany, to his Victorian home and suburban wife in Round Lake, the Warden's mind lingered on this Beauvais woman. She had struck some lost chord in him, an admiration of feminine power. While driving, he dictated into his tape recorder to research more about the history of the mines and to visit Heidi Beauvais again. After all, if her property abutted the seventeen acres of Fisher Hill Mine, he should know as much as he could about her and her ranch.

The 21 Mine

South of Whitehall, he turned right on Route 149, heading west, finally hitting the Northway at Exit 20, where he goosed it up to eighty mph, knowing no trooper would give him a ticket. They were in the same racket. Which reminded him that his paycheck should be in the mail. Never would he have imagined that every two weeks, a Puerto Rican immigrant like himself, would open an envelope with a New York State check made out for $4070.

He smiled and inserted a Gloria Estefan CD in his black Jeep Cherokee Limited. Molding comfortably into his leather seats, he sped home. He dreamed that maybe this final job would be more interesting than he anticipated. He could handle being around a gypsy woman who painted pictures and ran a ranch. He was fed up hanging around men who were quitters and took no responsibility for their lives of crime.

He was so relaxed and lost in the music and the imagery in his mind that at first he thought the ringing was part of the background to the CD. Quickly he realized otherwise, clenched his teeth, and answered his cell phone. His worst fear had occurred. Klocks had escaped. He shook his head in disbelief, and switched on the blinking red light inside the back window, keeping an eye out for the next 'No U-turn' sign.

Jeff Kelly

seven

Damian Houser was looking out the third story window of his squad bay. He was a day away from freedom, and he was scared. It was Thursday. On Friday, Damian would have to create his own reality, apart from prison. He knew if he went down to Harlem without a job, with no direction of his own, he would be drawn back into the drug scene.

He needed a new life. Damian was smiling at the view of the evergreen hills and the azure lake. It all looked prettier now that he knew he was leaving, back to the Big Apple, he supposed. Back to where his soul brothers were playing basketball and dealing drugs, and one real brother was working for his Dad's ad agency.

Compared to the other inmates from the city, Damian was intelligent and gentle. He grew up in a reddish brownstone on 110 West 127 street, next to PS 154, the Harriet Tubman Elementary School where he went to grade school. His father wore a suit to work, downtown to Madison Avenue with all the white folk at an advertising agency called Ogilvy & Mather.

Dad taught Damian that it's a white world out there, and rather than fight it, best to get along. Dad showed him the white man's handshake, firm and rigid, almost military like. Nothing like soul brothers who just make contact, brush by all loose and relaxed, no tight muscles, smiling, smooth, ready to move around at the slightest impulse.

It was that kind of background that had some brothers in prison saying Damian didn't belong here. That he was a middle class intellectual and too soft. Because he was a soul brother, the Bloods kept an eye out for him, knowing he was a short timer, and knowing that he got railroaded for selling a couple of ounces of pot. Before the mandatory sentencing of the Rockefeller drug laws, selling pot would have gotten him the same slap on the wrist that the white boys got. His counselor Thomason estimated that if you eliminated the drug-related convictions, two prisons in the Adirondacks would have been sufficient, instead of eighteen.

When he was sent Upstate, his hair had been in dreadlocks, a rebellious and stylish jab at his father. Damian fondly recalled the Saturday he had summoned the courage for his thirty dollar Caribbean dreadlocks and absentmindedly ran his hand over his head, expecting to feel his braids. Instead he rubbed his hand over the mandatory prison brush cut which was now growing out. Damian didn't know whether he'd ever again wear his hair long enough to be braided.

"Eyeballs!" a man in a tie said loudly at him. Damian was late for his last session, and Thomason, the prison counselor, had come to get him.

Startled, Damian awoke from his reverie, and automatically stood straight, and yelled the required response, "Snap, sir!" At one time or another, the rest of the squad had all been there, lost in time, back in a better day.

Thomason commuted down from the High Peaks in Lake Placid to the Adirondack foothills in Mineville, and was in command when A.D. was gone. He was the only other employee at Moriah Shock who wore a tie. Thomason used to work as a guidance counselor at Plattsburgh State University, but switched into the prison system when he saw how much he could make. Now his salary of fifty-one thousand was triple what he had been making as a college counselor.

"Damian, you need to get away from the environment that sent you here. Otherwise you'll be back," Thomason said, leaning forward across his desk.

"Easier said than done."

"How long has it been since you've seen your father?"

"Three years. I don't need to see him."

The 21 Mine

"Is he still in the city?"

"Still in the city, in the same ad agency, with another woman."

"So what are you going to do when you get out?"

"I'm working on it."

"That tells me you've got no plans. Think about this. Think about going somewhere else other than Harlem, especially since it'll be summertime. Statistics say our population does better in a new setting, rather than returning to the old setting, where you're surrounded by the same dope-dealing friends that got you here."

"Dissing my friends, eh." Damian used his new found prison discipline to let the insult slide by. "Okay, I'm not arguing. I'll come up with something. I've still got one day."

Thomason unlocked the door and Damian stepped out to walk back unescorted to D wing for the weekly community rap session.

Where would he be three years from now, three weeks from now? He passed Klocks in the hallway escorted by two guards back to his holding cell. Klocks gave him a peculiar all-knowing look that Damian wasn't sure of. The thing they had in common was that Klocks was a short timer too.

Whether Klocks had been sensing the future or not was hard to say, but on Saturday, the day after their fight over Chantal, Klocks walked up to Damian, offered him his hand and apologized - something he had never done before. Perhaps the truce was motivated by the knowledge that they were both being released shortly, Damian in less than a week and Klocks in a month. As happens with persons on the wrong side of the law who cross each other, from that handshake onward, they coexisted in a kind of shaky truce.

Damian tried not to alter his step, or the energy required to walk, but his body dripped with the uncertainty of his mind. He shoved open the door to the outside and looked up at his platoon flag beneath the stars and stripes, snapping against the flagpole, sounding like the rigging of a sailing ship. He wished that he was on a sailboat, reading the compass heading, listening to weather reports and choosing the right southern port. He needed a journey to take him away, a destination, a port of call for the next year of his life.

Jeff Kelly

Maybe Thomason was right. Harlem would be unwise, too much time and too few options, a rerun of a grade B movie with the final scene in a grade B prison. He drifted back to the one thing he had enjoyed the most at prison, working at the ranch. Maybe, until he got a plan, he could get hired at the ranch and see more of Chantal and her brown skin. Maybe Billy, the guard, or even Warden A.D., would help him. Had he just come up with a plan? The sun was shining as he walked into the dorm. He gave his pass to the security officer and just like in school, took a seat in the back row.

"And why do you have to pay taxes?" the teacher asked. Two inmates raised their hands. The first, a black man with a graying beard, said, "So our white government can oppress nations of color by waging war." The second answered, "So we can eat pizza in prison," and everyone, including the teacher, laughed.

* * * *

By the 1990's, the Adirondack region in general was viewed as the Adirondack Park or the Adirondack Prison Gulag depending on whether you were coming here to climb mountains or do time. Downstate in the city, the cold desolate Adirondacks was known as the Siberia of New York, and referred to simply as Upstate. Every denizen of the inner city, every young Black and Latino gang member, every white drug dealer or pot smoker, knew somebody Upstate - a region denigrated yet glorified in the gangster rap songs of Tupac, Gansta Rap, and Wu-Tang Clan. They rapped about going "Upstate," doing time "Upstate." If you were Upstate you were in prison.

A soot-covered bus, with the words UPSTATE TOURS in large letters above the windshield, would pull in tomorrow at 1:00 p.m. from the Port Authority. Through the windows, you would barely be able to make out the sleeping silhouettes of women, mostly black mothers, making their biweekly pilgrimage Upstate to visit their once innocent boys, to stand by their man.

If he wanted, Damian could ride back down to the City with the women, getting off at 34th Street to take the uptown A train home to 125th street. No, he'd take the local AA train, hear more of the sounds, see more of the sights, the characters he missed. He shut his eyes. He heard the rumble of the subway, the hard luck story of a beggar. He wanted to toss a quarter into a hat, while a panhandler hummed away on the harmonica. He saw the hot dog venders; he saw the nodded-out crack heads, he saw his sister on the stoop knitting a sweater the size of a man's hand for her baby, Rachel. He knew the rounds of the po-po, and recalled that he liked one of the cops.

He could do with a little ghetto life, the summer sizzle of a city, the scent of a woman, but he tried not to think about that. He blocked that out. He tapped his hard stomach, happy about the physical shape he was in from regular meals, regular work, early rising and early to bed. And he was also deliriously happy to be getting out, to put this episode behind him.

But really, what would he be going back to, but his past, which had put him here in prison. He was young. He still had a future. Where else could he go? He had twenty-four hours to decide, and just like in the movies, he was scared about all the freedom. About not knowing where to be when. No whistle blowing to start and stop work. He was used to following orders and needed direction.

* * * *

In the winter these Adirondack mountains had been so cold, and so uninviting, that even the guards referred to the prisons in the Adirondacks as a Siberian gulag. He remembered the day in early February, in the morning around 5:30 a.m., when the thermometer outside the window read 33 degrees below zero. He couldn't believe it. Until he had been shipped Upstate, he had never experienced a day below zero. Never in his life. That cold morning after breakfast, Billy announced to his platoon that a place forty miles west, called Blue Mountain Lake, was the coldest spot in the nation at 39 below. Damian shook his head in disbelief, the way Billy seemed excited by the extreme cold. Damian shivered thinking about it, and even got scared when his nostrils stuck together as they marched to breakfast. On the way back, Randy had said "Watch this."

Randy flung a looping slug of spit into the dry air, and when it landed on the macadam, it turned to ice. "Eh? Eh?" Randy repeated, as if to say, what do you think of that? Amazing thought Damian, worried about something called frostbite, his hands thrust in mittens, his ears covered by earmuffs.

Now, only three months later, it was as if he was on another planet. It was hot out, and he was warm in his green jacket. He took off his jacket and placed his sandals in the prescribed spot on the floor at the end of his cot. Once again, he gazed out the window into the evening sun. He heard a loud call outside, a deep cuk-cuk-cuk, and waited until he saw some movement and a red crest, and the largest woodpecker in North America, the pileated, flew away. Never before had he paid attention to a bird.

He was arranging his shelf, according to the precise posted regulations shown in a large picture on the wall, when a ladybug landed in the prescribed space between his toothbrush and comb. Suddenly, with one day left, the warm weather, the birds and bugs of spring, made the mountains around Moriah Shock seem like a better place to be. The only thing that was missing was a girl, and a few other people sporting the same nappy brown hair as Damian.

Damian let the lady bug be. There was a time he would have killed it. He looked in the mirror at himself. Who was he? His Betty Boop tattoo on his shoulder was a tribute to his mother, Betty, who basically had raised him alone, and wanted him back home with her in Harlem. Other than that, no identifying scars. In slow motion he pronounced his name in the mirror. "Damian Houser." He turned away from the mirror and proceeded to get permission to return to Thomason's office.

On a sunny day like this, which seemed almost miraculous to someone who had only experienced the shortened gray days of their Siberian winter, he decided he should spend his first few days of freedom right here, at the ranch and near Chantal, a stranger upon whom he had placed mythic importance.

"Some place else, doesn't mean here," Thomason said, somewhat perturbed. "Just because this woman spoke to you. She may have felt sorry for you. I can't stop you, but I advise you against it. I don't think we've ever released an inmate who's stayed around here. Not a black inmate, anyway."

Damian reached across the pine desk, and gave Thomason his firm, white man's handshake. He even looked the counselor in the eye. "Thanks for your advice. I hope we don't see each other again," he said with a grin.

eight

That night, Klocks crossed the paved Lincoln Pond Road running into the fields and woods and down the remnants of a logging road until he could no longer look back over his shoulder and see the dim outline of Moriah Shock. He slipped farther into the woods, startled two grouse, and slowed at a large beech tree carved with initials. He stopped there, panting with his head down, his hands against the smooth bark. He put his arm through the strap of his Nike bag, pushed off and trotted along a sandy path made by all-terrain vehicles.

Guided by the light of a gibbous moon, he locked in on a twinkling ribbon glowing through the blowing pines, reflections of an eight foot high, chain-link fence. Following the sandy path, he zigzagged closer, troubled only by a barking dog, and chose a spot next to a no trespassing sign where a birch tree grew entangled in the fence.

He expected to be followed, so he wasn't bothered by his tracks in the sand. He calculated he had until early morning before they came after him. But the barking dog was distracting him, and if the dog didn't stop, he might have to go back and kill it. No dog was going to sabotage his plans.

He unzipped the side pocket of his bag, and again put on the pilfered work gloves. In his mind he rechecked the details of his plan. Satisfied, he glanced around and tossed the bag over the fence.

He waited for the wind to come up and mask the noise. Using his left hand, he reached up and grasped a small branch that had grown into and around the three rows of barbed wire supported by cantilevered arms. He jumped up and grabbed a steel arm with his right hand, hoisting himself up until he was able to put his foot in a crook of the tree.

With acrobatic grace, he leaped from the tree and vaulted the fence, pushing down with his one gloved hand on the top row of barbed wire. It was spring, and he landed in a patch of corn snow. He stayed squatting for a few seconds, listening. Once up, he wove in among the aspen and pin cherry trees, pleased at how much light was thrown off by the moon.

Not far from the fence, he avoided a depression, sloped in front of him, but steeper elsewhere. Near the edge, he carefully stepped around coils of thick, two-inch cable, half-buried in the earth. He veered off for another twenty yards, until he saw bushes slanted downwards, and the ground underneath severely undercut. Again, he backed off from the edge of another drop-off, tripping over three sturdy bolts sticking up out of the ground, probably once used to secure cable. Wary of these uncharted sinkholes, he activated his mind's eye to recall the details of the aerial photographs in Warden A. D.'s office. Raising his knees and placing each foot straight down, he marched in slow motion in the direction of the disappearing horizon.

When the moonlit sky opened up before him, Klocks knew he had arrived. He put his bag down and stood tall at the edge of a great pit. The blasted out 21 Mine was much larger than he had envisioned. The pit was so big it was a canyon, three of its walls four hundred feet drops. Years ago, miners had blown away the earth to open up five separate tunnels at varying depths.

Across the abyss, the moon reflected off a metal roof of the town garage. The rock face below the roof was a sheer drop. A jumble of house-size boulders, blasted or tumbled down from above, were jammed up at the base, guarding the openings to the three deepest mines.

Klocks knew he must anticipate and avoid danger in order to find the safest route down the vast 21 pit to the tunnels at the base. He calmed himself for the descent while engaging all his nocturnal, animal instincts. Only as a last recourse would he use his flashlight. He knew what lay ahead.

Klocks was accustomed to succeeding where other men didn't. The execution of Klocks' bizarre plan hinged on his keen mental state, physical toughness, and will power. He was clever, he had less to lose, and he could activate a will that crushed all obstacles in his path. These traits were in tune with his ultimate instrument, his body - hard and resilient at 5'8" and 155 pounds, and accustomed to deprivation. But blessed as he was, Klocks recognized that to conquer the mines, he would need plenty of luck.

Klocks stilled the tension rising within him, and began his descent. The walls of this mammoth pit were either cliffs of solid rock or banks of loose stone called scree. When his heel slipped out from under him, pebbles skittered down the canyon. He followed a broken line of scattered bushes and aspen trees, figuring they clung to places he could cling to. Wherever possible, he held on to the trunks, no more than a few inches thick.

From across this man-made canyon, Klocks heard a call, a mournful and foreboding "caw caw," warning whatever lived or roamed in these long-neglected tunnels of an intruder. During the day ravens soared and tumbled high above the jumble of boulders, yet still well below the rim of the pit. The 21 Mine was that enormous. At night the adults served as sentries guarding their fledging ravens nesting on the cliff ledges. The only other known inhabitants of the 21 Mine were bats. Neither ravens nor bats were his favorite symbols of freedom, but Klocks reminded himself they were free nonetheless. When the ravens clucked again, Klocks felt the darker side of freedom and sensed an evil setting. He didn't want to die. He wanted to execute his plan and find another way out of the mines.

"You ain't seen nothing yet," Klocks said out loud, as if to answer the voices of the croaking ravens. "Tomorrow, the horde will descend."

Klocks was awed by the rakish forces of man and nature that called him forward to his destiny in the mines. He squinted directly across the pit, maybe eight hundred feet away, at two tunnels separated by a massive pillar of iron ore. Teardrop openings, the size of locomotives on end separated by a wide pillar, stared back at him like hypnotic eyes. Klocks thought they must be the original tunnels of the Harmony Bed.

He collected himself and turned his body so that he was facing the earth, and continued climbing down, slipping and sending rocks, some the size of bowling balls, careening off the crisscrossing ravines, kicking up other rocks on the way, until a landslide roared to the bottom. The echoes of the slide froze Klocks. When the noise subsided, Klocks harnessed his adrenaline and began moving again, this time descending with slower, surer steps, always striving for three points of contact.

The puffy moon showing off its own craters glowed overhead. Klocks knew that once inside the mines, he would have to use the flashlight and eventually the candles in his bag. The bag was essential to his escape, his complete disappearance.

Every fifteen feet he stopped to pick out the next cluster of small saplings, which would grow only where there was soil and less of a decline. He strained his eyes, trying to determine the angle and depth of the drops, making sure he wouldn't get rimmed and slide down a drop that led nowhere, unable to get back up.

At the very bottom of the blasted-out 21 complex, a glacier pushed against the undercut cliff. There the pit was shielded from the sun by towering rock faces and overhanging cliffs and covered in an insulating silt which preserved the ice. Four-story boulders and triangular ridges of hardened snow blocked the huge cliff-dwelling opening, where three large tunnels lurked, each with deep, vertical shafts. The rock sides of these dark tunnels were encrusted in snow. From the ceilings, icicles the size of leafless, upside-down trees guarded the inner blackness, glowing in the moonlight like jagged-toothed ghouls.

In the spring and summer, the silt-encased glacier poured water into the hungry tunnel openings. Inside the tunnels, 2000 foot vertical shafts, originally engineered to supply fresh air and power to the miners, filled with snow melt and rainwater, week after week, year after year, until the rising waters overflowed into the drifts, sometimes breaking through to another maze of tunnels in one thunderous gush, rattling the dinner dishes high above in the homes of Witherbee and Mineville.

Klocks knew from the prison librarian that most residents of Mineville were worried about 'the big one'. The big earthquake or the big sink hole that would open up and swallow their home like a mammoth earthworm from Hades. Near disaster hit on October 7, 1983, when an earthquake registering 5.0 on the Richter scale struck the Adirondacks. The epicenter was close to Mineville, thirty miles to the west in the town of Newcomb. The earth didn't open up, but it gave the locals above and around the 21 Mine something more to worry about.

Klocks cocked his head, half-listening for the fire whistle to signal an escape. He was proud to say this would be the first escape since the facility opened ten years ago in 1989. He correctly anticipated that the press and prison officials would be baffled why a man would want to escape with only one month left on his sentence. But his state of mind was dictated by his dread of the Chinese Mafia, and the breaking of an agreement with the Feds.

The calling of the ravens propelled Klocks onward and downward. The canyon of the 21 Mine was filled with sounds as if it were a living beast. The sounds of water and the moaning wind became Klocks' constant companions. Gurgling rivulets tumbled all around, slurping streams washing mud and iron ore residue off the eroding banks, depositing piles of silt to the glacier-like flow at the base. No longer was he buffeted by the warmer wind from the air above. What he did feel and hear was the blowing of cool air coming up from the bottom of the pit, air-conditioned by the glacier of ice, sand and snow.

He considered crisscrossing down on the left, but that might have left him stranded on a high promontory, so he chose right, where the vegetation stopped and the decline continued over smooth brown rock, instead of the crumbling sandstone. He felt more secure on the hard rock, with less chance of becoming part of a landslide.

He showed the confidence and experience of a rock climber, holding himself out away from the rock. He searched for holds with more friction. The deeper he descended, the more he felt like he was entering another environment, a trench or crater on the moon. He arrived at the smooth brown face, with no loose stone about and saw that he had misjudged the drop. It was steeper than he dare slide and higher than he dare jump. He thought about going back up and trying the other route, but that was not his nature.

The bag was hampering his descent, throwing off his balance, flopping between his body and the cliff face. He decided that, temporarily, it would have to go. He carefully tossed it down the same route he planned to take, and it tumbled over and over, slowly picking up momentum until it stopped half-submerged in one of the many muddy rivulets spreading downwards toward the mines.

He pictured his food and matches getting soaked and that rattled him. He hugged the rock and hurriedly scraped down, sliding, and then slipping and falling, as if he were glissading on snow, until he rolled over a ledge. He was twirled onto his back and slammed to a stop on top of the glacier. He lay still waiting for pain, puffing out his cheeks, exhaling a long breath.

Upon stumbling up, his right ankle hurt and he hopped toward his bag. He flipped the bag out of the trickling water, and fumbled inside for the flashlight. It still worked. He shined it on his Riddell boots, and saw blood. He hobbled onwards, walking on top of the glacier toward the chunks of ice that had been forced upward by the tremendous pressure. Above him, a third of the way up the sheer cliff, it seemed the eyes of the twin caves were watching him.

He lowered his eyes to concentrate on his own footing among the glittering magnesium iron ore and the larger angular rocks fallen from above. A gust of warm air washed over him, some inexplicable down draft off the tall cliff. He looked straight up at the endless rock wall, shrouded at the top in a plume of mist, and felt awe. The water cascading down the sides, and the cold air blowing out of the caverns colliding with the occasional warm gust from the canyon rim, transfixed him; the sound, the look of it all, almost made him believe that in nature was a sort of God.

The size and shape of the cavernous opening covering the tunnels reminded him of an ice age version of the cliff dwellers in New Mexico. Looking back up, he saw with satisfaction that, without the use of ropes, he had taken the only possible way down the canyon.

Then he heard the howls, the yelping of dogs on a scent, and high on the rim he saw lights - the streaking beam of flashlights, little darting comets. They had come for him. The guards were after him. They hadn't waited for daylight, after all. Someone must have spotted the open vent or the pieces of cardboard hanging from the razor wire. Surely, they'll wait until sunrise to descend. He had little time to waste.

nine

Damian was free, preceding Klocks by a setting sun, walking away from Moriah Shock down the hill to the corner store to buy a pack of gum, or a package of M&Ms, or maybe some smokes; he hadn't decided which.

Damian strode past a Guns n' Ammo sign on the left, followed by a Deaf Child sign, and then on the right Gloria's Restaurant. He walked fast, conditioned by the military tempo of Moriah Shock.

Gloria's was the restaurant Warden A.D. had told him about - $6.95 all you can eat, homemade pies, everything, but Damian had decided that his first stop, which was just coming into view, would be the corner store. He slowed his pace, reminding himself that he was free, and picked out the date of 1909 set in concrete beneath the slate roof.

The distinguishing feature of the Mineville store was a second story porch with curvaceous concrete spindles supporting the railing. The entire store was made of concrete block from the iron ore tailings with the rough side facing out, much like the row of gambrel-roofed bungalows nearby on Wall Street, built by Witherbee Sherman and Company in the flush mining years of the 1900's.

Damian lingered on the front stone steps of the Mineville Rexall Pharmacy, reading the labels on the glass door, feeling comfortable at a neighborhood store, really not too different from a corner store in Harlem. Next to the push sign, a sticker said 'If you smoke please try Carlton.' The drugstore clerk stared at him.

Damian thought the townspeople probably knew right off who he was. That he was a released inmate.

Once he asked where Witherbee was, she loosened up. "Oh, it's just a stone's throw away. Noticing his bag, she asked, "Are you walking?"

Now it was his turn to stare. She looked like an aged barbie doll, beehive blonde hair set off in a flip with pink, unblended circles of rouge on porcelain cheeks, and a little red bow under her white collar.

She was accustomed to pauses and wasn't annoyed by this young man not answering her question right away. In a moment, he snapped out of his reverie, "Yes, yes I'm walking." He continued to wander around the store, pleased at all the colors and candy, stopping to touch a cold pot-belly stove.

On weekdays, after eight o'clock, she didn't have many morning customers. Earlier in the morning, there was the crunch of guards coming in for coffee before driving up the hill to the prison, and loggers stopping before driving down the hill to the Ti Mill, but after that not much. There wasn't a TV and to pass the time she liked to chat.

"How far you come from?"

"Just up the hill," he said tentatively.

"Up the hill, at the prison?" she asked.

"Yes ma'am, up the hill at the prison." He waited for her response.

"How do you like it? How's the food?" It occurred to him that maybe she thought he worked there.

He had opened his M & M's and was eating them in front of her one at a time. Instead of answering, he offered her one, held between his thumb and forefinger. It was a yellow one.

"Oh, thank you," she said holding out the palm of her hand. He placed the M & M in her hand. She hesitated, and after a slight shudder of apprehension, popped the pill in her mouth. She had sold him the package, so it's not like she didn't know where the little yellow thing had come from. She sucked on the candy and smiled. She was puzzled by her passing moment of fluster, and didn't know what to attribute it to. Maybe she had been worried about hygiene. She couldn't have rejected his offer; that would have been insulting.

The 21 Mine

Damian hadn't forgotten her question. "The food was fine. Not as good as my ma's. But the price was right." Damian smiled back. "Do you want another one? A red one?" He chuckled as he picked it out. Something about being free made sharing candy fun.

"Okay, sure, one more. Thank you."

Damian could tell she was nervous. But she was pleasant, and that made his first half hour of freedom even better. He explained that the green van he rode in had passed right by her store every day, and he had promised himself that one day he'd walk in there and buy something. Today was that day.

To Damian, the nice thing about the store clerk was that she never asked him what he was in for. Usually, that was the first question he got. His answer was always the same, "inhaling." Point of fact, though, was that he was in for selling weed, not just smoking it.

After giving directions to Witherbee - "straight-away down the road," she volunteered one piece of advice. "Stay away from that big fenced-off pit. It's on the right. You won't see it. But you might hear it. I do, from my porch. I hear the sounds of cave-ins and ravens."

"I stand forewarned, my dear," he said pleasantly. Drifting over to the 'The Chewer's Choice - Skoal' sign, he pulled open the door and said his last "Bye Ma'am."

She was warming up to him just as he was leaving. That's always the way, she thought wistfully, ruminating on her single status - but only for a moment. That's all the time she would permit herself to waste on what might have been. She looked down at her hand where his fingers had touched her palm. That evening on the porch, she told her sister, "That's the first black man that's ever touched me." She said it in a straightforward tone, revealing neither pride nor prejudice nor longing. It was simply the only real event that had occurred that spring day at the store; May 7, 1999.

The dawning fact that he was an inmate, a prisoner, was secondary to her. She knew that without the prison to take up the slack from the closing of the mines, her Mineville Pharmacy would have been out of business long ago.

Damian emerged from the store, closed his eyes and raised his face to the sun. It was one of the few times he had felt warm in the six months since he had been recruited for Moriah Shock. He walked left on Hospital Road, the direction she had told him, toward the post office and the firehouse.

A Dodge king cab and a Camaro cruised up to the three way intersection. It was almost noon and a shift change at the prison. Soon all the guards would hear about the prisoner who had refused the free bus ride back to the Port Authority.

The guard in the truck looked right through him as he drove by, and a momentary case of nerves fluttered in Damian's gut, as if he had been caught doing something wrong. Then, the guard in the Camaro gave him a wave, and Damian felt downright relieved. He was skittish today, like a colt who has graduated to a larger paddock.

Damian moved onwards and ate the last three M&Ms, crumpling the little bag in his hand, ready to toss it. He straightened his back and remembered how sore it had been from leaning over to pick up all those empty six packs on North Country roads these last six months and instead shoved the M&M wrapper in his pocket.

A person was walking toward him from the direction of Witherbee. Damian squinted, holding his hand up to his forehead to shade his eyes. A woman was coming his way, a woman and a dog.

In time, they passed each other, and she said hi, and Damian said hello, and he was breathless inside. She was like a ghost, stunning him with a sighting. She had a mane of whitish, blonde hair, slightly darker in the middle, and wore a matching outfit of a faded blouse and shorts made of some patterned, silky-brown gossamer material, and red wool socks. All in all, an odd, but tantalizing image. Definitely, not what he'd expected to find strolling the back roads of the Adirondacks.

She was walking side by side with an Alaskan malamute. After they were a safe distance past, Damian looked back and watched her, feeling he should have said more than hello, unaware that she was Heidi Beauvais's oldest daughter, and that he had once fought over her sister, who was now the mistress of his dreams.

The twelve o'clock siren of the Fire House startled him and he resumed his pace, determined to show some discipline and reach his goal of Port Henry by the end of the day. A half mile later, the houses of the village of Witherbee

The 21 Mine

dotted a hillside above a decimated mining valley. From afar, the village looked old-fashioned and storybook. He heard the whir of a chainsaw mingled with the soothing sound of wind chimes. There wasn't another car or person in sight.

Across the road from where he stood, a North Country Community College sign pointed up the hill to one large white building, about two hundred yards away. He thought, hey yeah, I've always wanted to go to college. He was feeling giddy and curious about what it cost to enroll, now that he had earned his high school equivalency diploma, his G.E.D. He padded the folded white envelope in his front shirt pocket. It held all the money he had made at Moriah Shock at forty-five cents an hour, minus what he had spent at the prison store. A total of one hundred and twenty-three dollars.

His required yellow S.M.A.R.T. booklet stuck out of his back pocket. Required until today, that is. He remembered at least one thing from being drilled on the contents. 'Goals are: Specific, Measureable, Attainable, Realistic, Timely.'

He trudged up the hill, pushing down on his thighs with his hands. An eight feet steel mesh fence topped with barbed wire ran alongside the road, reminding him of the fence surrounding the grounds of Moriah Shock. 'No Trespassing' signs were posted every twenty feet. He blithely flung the yellow book over the fence and then looked beyond to where the earth disappeared. Two large black birds rode a plume of mist before diving back down into the abyss. Those must be the ravens, and that must be the pit the woman in the store warned me about, Damian thought. The sight brought back his fear of heights and he quickened his pace toward the parking lot.

One car was in the lot, and Damian noticed that somebody was sitting in it, staring at him. Trying to ignore the guy, Damian walked by him and up the steps to the front door of the building. The door turned out to be locked. Damian shrugged and from his higher perch, took in the view of the village, the woods, and two small gray mountains totally devoid of vegetation. As happy as he was, the overall view was hilly and harsh with patches of snow in the ravines facing north. Beyond the fenced-off hillside that he had walked up, the jagged top edges of a vast pit, many times larger than a football field, stared back at him.

From the parked car, the driver turned to him and said, "The college is closed. I come here to eat lunch and catch the view." He held up a paper bag to show he was eating lunch. The driver was old and had the pale, white skin of a hospital patient.

Next to the driver's sandwich bag, Damian eyed a can of beer, a brand he didn't know - Genesee. Damian hadn't drank a beer since he had been incarcerated, and though he was never much of a beer drinker, he longed for a taste.

"Here, have some," the old man said, raising the can above the seat and out the car window.

Damian took a swig. "What's behind the fence?"

"The old 21 Mine. They shot down the roof in 1877, and made it into an open pit."

"It seems kind of eerie."

"Yeah, in a way, it is."

"And those gray hills over there?"

"Iron ore tailings. Where you from? You from the prison?" the old man asked. Locals were told not to refer to Moriah Shock as a prison, but they did anyway. They got a chuckle out of the phrase correctional facility. Few believed in the concept of change, and certainly not change for the better.

"Yep. That's where I'm from, today."

"I can tell that. There ain't but one or two black folk who live in all of Essex County."

"I believe it," Damian said. Once he had accepted the beer, Damian figured he owed the man a conversation, and he was curious about this 21 Mine. Hadn't Klocks mentioned it to him once?

"I'm from Harlem."

"Where's that?"

Damian raised his eyebrows. He thought everybody had heard of Harlem. "It's in the city, Manhattan, the Big Apple." Damian assumed at the least, the codger had heard of New York City. "What about behind the fence? What do you know about it?"

The 21 Mine

The old man pushed his bologna sandwich aside, and opened the car door to stand in the sun next to Damian. The man had trouble getting up from his car seat, so Damian reached in and the man grabbed Damian's wrist, and Damian held his, pulling him up out of the car. In the process the man's cap fell off and Damian handed it back to him. It had a Republic Steel logo on it.

"The seat's too low," muttered the man, coughing.

By now the two of them were side by side on the Plymouth, leaning a few feet apart. Damian was happy just to be able to talk without being addressed as 'Eyeballs!' or hollering, 'Sir, this inmate requests permission to speak, sir!'

Once the old man cleared his throat and drank the last swallow of beer, he began to tell Damian about the mines. Damian knew he was in for a story of a bygone era, and thought the circumstances weren't much different from meeting an old man sunning himself on a stoop on the corner of 125th and Lenox. Damian decided he was in no hurry. He leaned back against the man's rusted Plymouth Valiant and listened.

"Yeah, I worked in all the mines. Old Bed up the hill, Harmony over there, Joker back over near Fisher Hill, near your prison, and the 21 Mine here. Stay here long enough and you might feel the ground shake. This whole area's undercut with shafts and tunnels.

"You wouldn't have believed this place back then. Before my time, your Fisher Hill and the Barton Mine here, and Lyon Mountain up north produced more iron ore than any other part of this country. Around 1895 I think. And that pit there, the 21 Mine, was the mother of them all."

"1895. Even before your time, eh," Damian said. "How old are you?"

"Me, I'm 79. The only reason I'm still alive is that I kept quitting the mines. Of course I never got seniority, but I didn't get silicosis either. That's because I took time off and got some clean Adirondack air in my lungs. Everyone else I worked with is dead." He paused to cough. "It used to be called miners' consumption."

"My grandpa who came here by freighter in the 1870's, worked right under your prison, at Fisher Hill. He died of miners' consumption in 1919. Christ, when I worked in the mill in the cellar, over the shipping bin, a 200-watt bulb four feet away was a faint glow. You wouldn't have believed the dust."

"During one of those little vacations of mine - 1941 I think, I was hiking in the Adirondacks. I was on the summit of Gothics, on a clear day, and I saw what I thought was smoke from a forest fire some thirty miles away, toward Lake Champlain. A couple of days later on the trail, I met a forest ranger and I asked him about the fire. He told me it wasn't a fire; it was dust from the iron ore mill at Mineville."

"Over there, you see the long roof on that green building. I used to clean up there. That's the change house for Harmony."

Damian was getting the feeling that these mines were nasty places. "These mines are all closed, right?"

"Republic Steel closed up shop in 1971. There was less and less mining each year. Tunnel mining was too expensive. Wasn't 'cost-effective,' they told us. That's why they collapsed the 21 Mine, hoping to get easier access to the iron ore. That's a mine you want to stay away from. There's blasted open stopes and shafts and drifts leading every which way. Families were afraid their kids would go down there and get lost or worse. That's why the forty thousand dollar chain-link fence. The steel posts are set in concrete and there's three stands of barbed wire on top. I know because I was hired in '79 to help seal the 21 Mine."

The old man's eyes got that far away look, as if just yesterday he was working down in the mines. "God, it was hard work. But, you know what, you felt proud and you slept like a baby."

Damian could tell this guy's whole life was the mines. "What did you do down there, in the mines?"

"I drilled. I operated a jackhammer. A drill with forged steel on the end. I used to weigh over two hundred pounds." He stared at Damian for a while. Finally, he asked. "How was it in prison?"

"Prison?" Damian repeated, looking up at the blue sky and then down at the barbed wire surrounding the pit, not ten yards from the car. "Prison wasn't half bad. I got my minimum, my year and a half sentence, cut to six months. Sounds like being sentenced to the mines was worse."

That comment crinkled the lines on the old man's face. Damian closed his eyes and tilted his head back. "Well, I'm going to continue my walk."

The 21 Mine

"One last thing. There was this screen actress, Pearl White. She starred in the movie, Perils of Pauline, way before your time. Yep, she tightrope walked on a cable strung one thousand feet over the open pit of the 21 Mine. It was quite a stunt."

"What, they set up a cable just for her?" Damian asked, as he looked in the direction of the gray birch trees blocking his view of the canyon.

"Oh, no. No, it was an inch and a half steel wire cable for a trolley and a bucket. From the center of that cable, miners used to be lowered right to the floor of the canyon to dynamite for iron ore. In the bucket. My dad once rode down in the bucket, carrying a box of blasting caps. The thing swayed like hell. He was scared to death."

Damian thought back to the day, six months ago, when he was scared to death, on his ride in a green correction bus headed Upstate. Both he and the old miner were quiet for a while. "Where you headed?" asked the old man finally.

"I want to walk through that village," Damian said as he shielded his eyes and pointed across the valley.

"That's Witherbee."

"And then I'm going into town and order some Chinese food."

"You mean down in Port Henry."

"Right."

"You need a ride then."

"No, I'm fine. I want to walk. If I wanted to ride, I would have taken the bus out of here. I'm not ready to go back to the city yet. Nothing's calling me."

"Okay, partner. Off Hospital Road take a left at Power House Road, and that will bring you into Witherbee, and then left by the Harmony change house, where I used to shower and clean up after work . They used to call that street Hog Alley. Port Henry is a ways down the hill."

Damian took the first few steps to leave, but the old man continued.

"The first building you'll see is a big stone structure. You can see the turret from here. It's the VFW. When it was called Memorial Hall, Republic Steel built six bowling alleys in the basement to entertain the miners. Here, back up, the fog's gone. Take a look."

"I do see it. Jesus, what's that on the lawn?" Damian asked.

"A rocket," commented the old man. "It used to mean something."

Damian didn't want to get him started again, and called out "Thanks," waving over his shoulder as he passed a corner of the fenced-off 21 Mine.

Damian walked past the chain-links puzzled by something. Lurking in his brain was the notion he had heard of the 21 Mine even before the store clerk's warning.

A raven rose up and glided away. Its deep, guttural croaking echoed off the plunging, rock faces, a melancholy wonk-wonk. He couldn't help but think of Klocks, and shook his shoulders, as if trying to shake off clawing hands. Hands trying to lure him, trying to bring him back down.

ten

Damian took the short cut the old miner pointed out. From the back of a yellow truck, guys in orange reflective vests were shoveling tar into pot holes leftover from another rough winter. The smell reminded him of hot summers in the city. He tipped his Mets cap to the men who nodded silently in return.

In the midst of two withered mining towns, on the corner of Silver Hill Road, he turned onto Witherbee Road. Across from the green change house, a man in a blue ski parka sat in a rocking chair on his porch, sipping something out of a paper bag. As Damian walked by, the man's arm rose in high salute.

He read the sign next to the abandoned change house, and gazed down in the hollow. The sign said Republic Steel Corp., Adirondack Ore Mines. 'Adirondack,' he liked the word. Billy, the guard told him it was an Indian word meaning barkeater. Damian was full of curiosity, at least for today, enjoying every oddity, straying into a town passed over by the technology of the 1990's.

Farther along the change house street, a woman sweeping her porch, stopped to stare at him. It wasn't a look of hostility, but it was a stare. He was coming to realize that staring must just be an Adirondack thing.

Downstate staring was an invitation to trouble. Upstate it was apparently just a provincial habit, a weird hello. In a rural county like Essex, strangers got stared at. That's all. She wasn't dissing him. It wasn't like on 125th Street where a baleful stare was an invitation to fight.

The woman had run a line of clothes from her tilted Victorian porch across a small creek to a maple tree. The blue jeans, cut off T-shirts and black denim pants looked to be about Damian's size and would have been easy for him to take. Maybe he'd just borrow them. She crossed her creaking porch, watching Damian as he watched her. The screen door slammed behind her. He hadn't heard a screen door slam in a dog's age and thought it a wonderful sound.

She reappeared, grabbed her broom, and sat down on her Kennedy rocking chair.

"What you looking at?" she called out.

Damian spun around to make sure there was no one behind him. But lo and behold, she was talking to him. He approached her porch. "What's the best way to walk to Port Henry?" he asked.

"Down the hill to Moriah Corners, where all them taverns is, and then straight down from there past the golf course." The wind gusted and her chimes sprinkled the air and softened the mood. He surprised himself by sitting on the porch steps.

"I heard you were coming this way," she said.

Now, that got his attention. "Helen called me from the pharmacy. We look after each other up here," she said rather smugly. "How come you ain't in prison?"

"They let me out, dummy," he said, mumbling the last word so she couldn't make it out. Then he felt bad, sensing she wasn't as hostile as she first appeared.

"Can I have one of those cut-off T-shirts?" he asked point blank.

She rocked faster and narrowed her eyes, holding the broom across her chest, like she might have to parry an attack.

"A cut-off T-shirt? That's what you want, eh?"

"Yes ma'am. All I have for clothes is what you see." Which wasn't exactly true, but almost.

"Stay there," she said pointing the broom at him. With surprising agility, she popped up out of the rocker, put the broom down across the arms of the chair, and hand over hand reeled in the clothesline. The dry clothes bobbed and raced across the little brook inches above getting wet.

The 21 Mine

She removed the clothespins from the largest of the sleeveless T-shirts. "Joey won't mind," she said as she folded it up, her hands flying, and pitched it right to him.

"Now get." She picked up her broom and felt secure again. "Get or I'll put a spell on you."

With those words, Damian almost tripped backwards on the steps. He laughed, but she had aroused the superstitious side of him. He did his best to ignore her comment and his own reaction, and put the T-shirt on right over his western-style, denim shirt. Looking back, Damian wasn't sure why he asked for the T-shirt. He just didn't know what to say, or even why he had approached her porch.

Beyond Lamos Lane off to the left, he passed an attractive church, made of the blocks from mine tailings, painted white, trimmed in patterned red brick. The church reminded him of some of the tidy neighborhood churches in Harlem.

He picked up the pace and in ten minutes came upon the other end of Silver Hill Road. He looked farther up the road at a large house that sat across from an open field and saw a Confederate flag flying. He didn't like the sight. It unnerved him. It let him know he wasn't in Harlem, that's for sure. But Damian had convinced himself that this was his day, his first day, and nothing was going to deter him.

A half hour later, he strode into Moriah Center, a haphazard five-way intersection with tilted stop signs rammed by snowplows, nearly touching the ground. The slanted sheds and crooked, closed bars hadn't been painted in years. With the exception of a plastic banner outside The Old Mine Saloon which read 'Welcome NasCar Fans' and a red, neon Budweiser sign glowing above a green three-leaf clover, the five corners had the feel of a back woods barrio that a good burst of wind could clear out, and all for the better. He couldn't find any charm in the place and walked downhill onto Dugway Road.

His motto for the day was 'keep on truckin.' Half hour later past a Y-intersection with Tarbell Hill Road, he stopped at a convertible parked in front of a boarded-up furniture store. It was a 1970 baby blue Cadillac Seville with a for sale sign. The body was in good shape, no rust that he could see, and he wanted to know if it ran. The sign said to inquire at 30 Forge Hollow Road at the next corner. So Damian took a detour, a jaunt, to ask about the Cadillac.

The Forge Hollow Road dove down and around a corner. In no time at all, Damian beheld a square house made of large stones, next to a sparkling creek running beside an abandoned railroad bed. It was a D & H railroad bed, which had been built with tons of rock from the mines. The sun lit up the valley which glowed like an African savanna, trees spread out among tall grass, crisscrossed with lilac bushes in bloom, a scent of flowers in the breeze. Its rhythmic order mesmerized Damian. He was about to knock on the recessed red door, when he saw bits of quartz crystal inset in the stone wall in the shape of the number 30 above a small chalk board. Written on it was today's date and the message, 'I'm out back working on the tanks.'

He drifted to the side of the house by a meticulously restored red Ford pick-up, with style-side fenders, mud on the tires, and a Marine Corps 'Semper Fi' bumper sticker on the back and a 'Vietnam Vet' sticker up front. Around the back of the house, between a stone patio and the river bed, Damian passed a cannibalized, ski-boa snowmobile and a black 1959 Mercedes Benz with fog lights but no windshield and no tires. At the far end of the field, loomed two large gasoline storage tanks.

He heard a crackling sound between the two tanks. A man wielding a torch, wearing goggles, was cutting out one end of a cylindrical tank eight feet in diameter. He had yet to notice Damian who stayed a safe distance away. Two hoses led from his torch to tanks of oxygen and acetylene above him in the bucket of his back hoe. When the flame went out, Damian heard music, something like acid-rock. The torch snapped when the man relit it, and in the process a corner of the man's glove caught fire. He was facing Damian now and flipped up his shield so he could put out the fire.

After patting out the fire with his other glove, he stood perfectly still, looking straight at Damian for a good thirty seconds. He walked over to the seat of the loader and turned off the boom box, and said "I'll be right with you." He winked at Damian and said, "Jimi Hendrix, Are You Experienced."

The man looked like an older fellow, probably sixty but trim and in good shape. He had white hair and his pink polka dotted cap was turned around backwards. He was wearing blue jeans, with the ruddy tan of someone who worked outside. Damian moved closer to see exactly what the man was doing with the torch. He was about to cut through the last few inches of iron around the edge of the bottom of the cylinder. In the middle of the circle he had already cut out a one foot by one foot square, and Damian could see that the whole damn thing was about to fall out. Damian grabbed a hold of the inside edge of the square to help hold the circle upright.

"Be careful," yelled the man. And then he pointed to another pair of gloves on the ground, which Damian reached down to pick up. He put them on and grabbed the opening again.

"It's going to be heavy," the man warned as he stepped back and shut off the torch. He picked up an over-sized, ball-peen hammer and slammed it against his last cut. Damian braced himself, but instead of crashing out, the eight foot circle of metal slipped down an inch inside the tank and swung there like a baffle. They could move the bottom in or the top out, but they couldn't pull the cut circle out of the cylinder.

"Forget about it. I'll drag it out with my loader." He put down his torch, gloves and goggles and stepped back. "I'm going to store firewood in these. I'll take off the other end so the air can circulate. And the tanks being dark, they'll absorb the sun and dry the wood."

"Where did you get them?"

"State regulations. All gas stations with buried tanks more than twenty years old have to get rid of them. It's putting the small stations out of business. It can cost up to a hundred thousand dollars to install a new one. By the way, I'm John."

"I'm Damian. I was at Moriah Shock. I just got released."

"How come you're hanging around?"

"I don't know. I might like it here now that it's warming up."

"Hmmm," John grunted.

"I saw the Caddy."

"Oh, I see. What did you do, rob a bank?"

Now it was Damian's turn to stare. "No, I didn't rob a bank. Not yet."

"Well, there's not much work around here. Not since the mines have closed, and that was years ago. Those used to be the tracks that took the ore to the barges in Port Henry."

"Yeah, that's where I'm headed today."

"It's not far. The Caddy is $4700, firm."

"Well I don't have the money today, but I plan to get it. And when I do, I'll be back. Does it run?"

"I'll get it running. Just needs a new battery. You give me a couple of days' notice when you're coming back and I'll have it purring for you, if you have the cash."

"It's a deal," Damian said. "But it might take me a few months."

"How long were you in for?"

"Six months."

"Drugs, right? Selling drugs."

"Yep, selling pot."

"Marijuana?" repeated John with an incredulous look on his face. "Why one of our school board members is a regular pot smoker. Hell, I can show you fields on the other side of the tracks where hippies have planted pot. That's it. Pot. You're lying to me."

"Nope. But you see what color I am, don't you. Hey, they threw me in jail while Daddy's lawyer got the white kid out."

John didn't say anything one way or another, and it was hard to know what he was thinking. He climbed into his loader and lowered the bucket.

"Give me a hand here, will you?" From the bucket, they lifted out one tank of oxygen and then one of acetylene.

"That's good. I can do the rest myself."

"Did you build that house?" Damian asked. They both stood among the equipment, arms crossed, legs spread, and looked across John's field.

"It was meant to be the pump house for a dam here on Mill's Creek, but it was never in operation. When I bought it, the roof was caved in. That was about 25 years ago."

"God, it's neat looking now."

"Yup. I put a lot of work in on it, right after I left the mines."

The 21 Mine

"Why did you leave?"

"Too dangerous. Too many accidents. Too many eye injuries. Too many foot amputations," he said as he attached a chain to his bucket and hopped back on his loader. "I got to get back to work."

"Jesus. Worse than prison."

"Way worse than prison. It seemed like miners died every year. Five in 1951."

As John shifted gears and the motor rumbled, Damian started to walk away. As a way of saying good-bye, he turned and called out, "How's the Chinese restaurant in town? I'm dying for Chinese food."

"The Golden Palace. The food's okay. But they might not take to you."

"Why not?"

"Well, you're not Chinese, and until this morning, you were in prison, right?"

Jeff Kelly

eleven

Damian tossed a wave to John on his loader from the middle of his field of dreams. Damian was struck by the directness of these mountain people, and he was getting accustomed to the prolonged staring.

He walked back up Forge Hollow Road to the Moriah Plank Road, where until 1869 horse drawn wagons had hauled iron ore down to the Cedar Point Furnace on Lake Champlain. Damian held his breath while walking past the graveyard opposite the golf course, whose greens had turned brown. As he got closer to the village of Port Henry, a few of the old buildings reminded him of the ornate brownstones in Harlem. The only difference was that here there weren't any people hanging around, especially no young people. Walking down what was quite a steep hill on Broad Street, he caught a glimpse of the lake. Billy had told him that you could take a boat from Port Henry north on Lake Champlain all the way to Montreal and the St. Lawrence River and out to the Atlantic Ocean. That struck him as kind of neat and fanned his feeling of freedom; an adventuresome attitude that carried him forward like a southerly wind catching his sails.

He had heard there was a diner in town, which might be a place where he could feel comfortable. Maybe he'd find a Daily News or a Post he could read. He wanted to find out about the New York City sports teams. Unlike medium and maximum prisons, Moriah Shock had no TVs and no newspapers.

On the sidewalk outside of Jimmy's, a movie theater converted into a corner store with lotto and porno magazines, Damian surveyed a rack of newspapers and bought the Daily News which had a photo of a forlorn Daryl Strawberry on the back. Damian paid from the money in his white envelope and crossed the street feeling more at home as he dodged one car and another braked for him. He knew where he was going with his paper - straight to the Golden Palace. It was about five o'clock and he was the only customer.

He felt the bills in his envelope and walked up to the counter. A young Chinese man, with a white chef's hat, and a tuft of straight, straw-like, black hair, scrutinized him from the kitchen behind the counter.

The screen door in the back of the restaurant slammed. Damian saw an even younger Chinese girl maneuver her bicycle into the back of the kitchen.

Damian waited for the Chinese man to approach the counter, but he just kept slicing mushrooms on a worn wooden butcher's block. The girl said something in Chinese, removed her scarf, and walked to the counter.

"What you have? You want dinner?" she asked.

"I want two pints of egg drop soup, chicken fried rice, and shrimp chow mein, all for here and an order of sautéed mixed vegetables."

She was writing on a piece of paper. "That's $16.33 with tax. You pay now."

Unless times had changed, Damian thought it was customary to pay after he received his food.

"I'll pay afterwards," he said, looking around.

Damian turned his back to the counter, in defiance, and looked out the picture window and the propped-open door. Of the six or seven persons he saw outside, one bearded man walked briskly by with an elongated stride, exaggerated arm swing, and a scowl on his face; one limped and slurred his speech; one adult was being led by another adult, holding hands as they crossed the street; one woman was drooling while she shouted at traffic and the apparitions of her mind; and two thirteen year old boys, Pepsis in hand, were examining baseball cards as they left Jimmy's. The kids appeared normal, but of the others he wasn't too sure.

The 21 Mine

Unbeknownst to Damian, some of the others lived in community residences sponsored and monitored by an agency called the Ark, which helped the less fortunate. Most lived across Main Street in the Lee House, formerly a grand hotel of the mining era, since renovated by the Ark. For their administrative headquarters, the Ark had bought an old brick Victorian building behind the Grand Union with the best view of Lake Champlain and the Crown Point Bridge.

In the early 1970's, after 1971 when Republic Steel closed the mines, but before the Stewart's Shop came to town, before the Ark took over the Lee Hotel, Port Henry was every shade of dirty gray. Cracked sidewalks and cracked souls collected unemployment or went on welfare, moving from one damp, dreary apartment to another, always owing back rent, never paying. The weather was lousy. In winter it was cold without snowing, and in summer it rained. The only tourists were social workers. By the 1980's and '90's, things had changed, were almost looking up, thanks in part to the Ark.

Damian figured maybe he'd fit right in, because certainly by small town, North Country standards, he was less fortunate too. He stepped outside and watched as a king cab up pulled up to the curb in front of the post office. On the driver's side of the door was printed "Bog Pond Ranch." Down stepped Heidi and her three hippie daughters, including the ghostly walker in the gossamer outfit, and Chantal, the youngest and last daughter to leave the truck. She saw Damian right away, gave a shy wave, and moved a few steps in his direction. She said something to her mother, and instead of following the clan into the post office, she walked up to Damian.

"I trust you're out and not AWOL."

"Does your mom mind you talking to me?"

"No, she doesn't care."

"Yeah, everyone's all surprised because I didn't take the bus back to the city."

"My sister told me she saw you out walking on the Hospital Road."

"Yeah," Damian said, all jittery, shifting his weight from one foot to the other, "The last time I saw you I almost ended up in the hospital." They both let out an embarrassed laugh. An awkward silence followed. Damian broke the lull by blurting out, "Do you need any help at the ranch? Like a hired hand? I could live in the barn or something. Paint all the fences. Do whatever you ask me to do. Think about it and ask your mother."

"I don't know what my mother would say. It might be all right with me. Well how do I get in touch with you?"

"I don't know. How about letting me know tomorrow, same time, Saturday at six. Right here at the Chinese restaurant."

"We come in town about every day. So I could probably work that. Where are you going to stay tonight?"

"I've hardly thought about it. I'm just trying to get a meal, but she," as Damian jerked his head toward the window, "wants me to pay first, before I get the food. Do you believe that?"

"That's just because she doesn't know you and she's paranoid."

Chantal explained that the Chinese here in the Adirondacks are from the Fukien province, which is a poor seaside province far away from cities like Shanghai or Beijing. These Chinese migrated to the ghetto within Chinatown, under the Manhattan Bridge. They're the poorest of the poor and watch every penny.

Damian was impressed with all her knowledge and felt thrilled to stand next to her. "How do you know all that?"

"I know all about the history of this place, plus I'm curious about anyone from the outside who lives inside this county. First, I learned a few words of Chinese. Then she started to trust me. In exchange for the little English I taught her, she answered all my questions about her world. You know what?" Chantal lowered her voice and leaned closer. She whispered, "The Fukienese are smugglers."

Chantal grabbed Damian by the shirt cuff and led him inside. She spoke the Fukienese dialect to the woman behind the counter and then introduced Damian. Damian bowed slightly, and it seemed the confrontation was over.

Chantal turned to Damian and whispered. "You have the money, right?"

"Yes, I have it," responded Damian somewhat defensively.

"She's cooking your order now. Wait, wait." Chantal saw her mom through the glass window and ran out the door to tell her she would meet her in fifteen minutes around the corner at the bank.

The 21 Mine

She ran back inside, pleased to have found some action, something unexpected going on in her beloved, but dreary Port Henry. "I'll buy you a Pepsi. How's that? This can be your celebration meal. Your freedom meal."

"Sounds great, but let me pay."

"No I'll buy the drinks, you buy the meal."

While Chantal and Damian were all starry-eyed, the Chinese girl was in the back of the kitchen talking to the Chinese man Damian had first seen in the store, and another older and heavier Chinese man with black hair and a white goatee. They huddled next to the cover over the grill and the muffling whir of the exhaust fan - because maybe Chantal knew more of the Fukien dialect than 'Hello, how are you?' The Chinese were having a heated discussion, constantly looking askance at Damian who, in the company of Chantal, was oblivious to their darting stares.

Then the Chinese switched to broken English and moved up front to the counter still jabbering. "Yes, he prison man."

"Aren't you prison man."

Now Damian pounced in on the discussion.

"Yes," he stood up. "I prison man. I prison man. But that's yesterday," he said grabbing his own clothes. "This is tomorrow. This here," fingering the table with his chopsticks, "is today. And I am free. Free as you are."

"Yes, yes, yes," they said nodding.

"But you prison man and you know Klocks."

Damian went wide-eyed at their knowledge of the name of another prisoner.

"Yes, see," they said pointing at Damian and his reaction, "You know Klocks. Klocks is not a free man, right. He still in prison, right?"

Damian leaned back and took a deep breath. "This is a small town isn't it," he said to Chantal. And then to the Chinese leering at him from behind the counter. "Right, Klocks is in prison, for now." Finally, Damian let out a "Aha," indicating recognition of why they knew Klocks. Of course, since the man Klocks assaulted in the kitchen was Chinese, the Port Henry Chinese had heard of Klocks, his assailant. Klocks had stabbed the wooden spoon in the chef's ear, so in a puppet-like gesture, Damian stuck a chopstick in his own ear and glared at the Chinese. That took a smile off their faces.

"What are you doing?" Chantal asked feeling slightly off balance as to what was going on between Damian and the Chinese.

"I'll tell you later. Don't worry about it. They know about this guy Klocks in prison, and I don't think they like him. But here we are and your fifteen minutes are almost up. Next time I'll buy the drinks - Champagne." He tapped his empty Pepsi down on the table and spun it around. "See what you can do for me. I mean I'll be no trouble. I just want to try something different - spend a couple of months in the country. Free in the country."

Every few steps on the sidewalk Chantal giggled a 'howdy' at the toot of a horn, or twirled to wave or as she chatted her way to Albank, which used to be US Trust, which used to be the Glens Falls National Bank. Her mom Heidi was inside objecting to the fact that she was receiving mortgage payment notices from some bank in Louisiana. Her local bank explained that they had sold her mortgage to another bank, and Heidi wasn't happy. Why use your local bank if you weren't going to get personal services? She preferred to pay in person and now she was pissed.

She threatened to take back her pastoral painting of silver birch and a swamp swathed in fog, a gaggle of geese flying overhead. Of course, the bank president had paid two thousand dollars for it. She looked at her painting and thought of her money flying south, along with the middle class Adirondackers who had pensions and could afford to take off for Florida each winter.

"Hi Heidi," Chantal said.

"Going, going, gone . . . that's my new motto. They sold my mortgage to some bank down south. I can't believe it. If I knew they were going to sell it, I would have shopped around for a cheaper rate. I would have used the goddamn Internet."

Heidi was already bummed because she had discovered the local shoe store no longer carried her favorite Tony Lama cowboy boots. 'Going, going, gone . . .' was all she could think about as she stomped out of the bank.

She jammed the pickup's stick shift into reverse, but had to wait while two men shuffled across South Main Street. In front of her on the curb a white-haired woman with a craggy, yellowish face, stood with a vacant look slowly turning her head from side to side, as old people sometimes do. It was as if she were surveying the horizon.

"She's probably wondering where the movie theater, the old bank, Kobel's meat market, and Sagan's clothing store, all went. Well, I'll tell you where they went. Going, going, gone . . . just like my mortgage. If I don't watch out, soon I'll be the confused one standing on the corner and nodding, wondering where everything went."

Chantal could see now was not the time to ask about the hiring of an ex-con as a ranch hand. Instead, she and her sisters, rolled down the passenger windows and started singing "Going, going, gone . . ." to the beat of Tina Turner's 'What's Love Got to Do With It.' Last summer they had all driven down to Saratoga to see Tina rock and roll and strut her stuff at age fifty something. Older than them but not older than their Mom. "Going, going, gone . . ." They drove up the Broad Street hill, past the Golden Palace, where Chantal and her sisters waved to a handsome, black man standing outside.

"Wasn't he on Billy's work crew?" Heidi remarked.

"He was," Chantal confirmed.

"What's he doing there?"

"He's free." Chantal took a chance and continued, "And he wants to work at the ranch."

"So that's where you disappeared to."

"Mom, you don't have to decide now."

"Thank you, honey," Heidi said sarcastically. "Girls, gimme some gum will ya," and they drove back up to Mineville.

* * * *

The next morning, on Saturday, after Chantal had thoroughly washed the dishes, she again broached the subject of Damian.

"Where's he going to sleep? He can't sleep in the house. Not with the girls." Heidi said, as she looked over at her stuffed red fox and continued painting.

"Heidi," Chantal said in exasperation. The girls all called their mother by her first name. That's the way she liked it too. Then the age difference was less obvious. Chantal could usually wear down her mom, to the point where it was just easier to give in and say yes, than to listen to Chantal sigh, and moan and cry. Basically anything to get her way. A trait she had learned from her mother when Chantal was a little girl, watching her Mom deal with her various men friends most of whom were younger than she. Chantal dared not utter the thought, but privately she worried about her mom trying to make it with young, black, virile Damian.

"Heidi, it's because he's black, a Negro right?" Chantal knew that statement would really annoy her, really get to her. Heidi prided herself on her unbiased liberalness; it was one way in which she showcased herself.

"That has nothing to do with it, and you know it. Do you see any other men living here? No, it's just us girls." The sisters were listening while one knitted a quilt, the other read Moby Dick, and Chantal squinted over a copy of Playboy, delighted to see the Olympic skater Katarina Witt in the nude with her big muscular thighs.

"Just us girls, Mom? That's just because you don't have a boyfriend now."

Heidi brushed a few forceful strokes, filling in the fox's trademark tail and didn't respond. Chantal had always been the first to challenge her, and in many ways was the most like her. If the other girls had disrespected her that way, she might have slapped them because it would have been so out of character. Chantal got away with more than the others because she was consistently pressing her and Heidi expected it.

Finally Heidi relented. She was not able to 'Just Say No' like Nancy Reagan, her philosophical opposite, preached. If anything, Heidi lived by the expression 'Just Say Yes,' and so far the family had survived, though each one of the three daughters was divorced. Heidi's love of painting, her notoriety and the necessity to live up to her own carefully cultivated image, kept her going.

In her adult life, she had never gone out with someone her own age, always younger; five years, ten years, once even twenty years younger. Up here in the mountains, a single woman, especially one with a little kick, got a lot of attention. She liked being driven to the taverns around midnight on a Friday or

Saturday with a man who bought her drinks. She saw her friends and they would come over and chat. She never stayed too long; just long enough to make an impression.

Of all the Adirondack artists, she was perhaps the most adventuresome, and summer people in the know from the city collected her work. Depending on the sex and age of the buyers, one of two styles of her paintings hung over their fireplaces. If a well educated younger or middle-aged New York City woman bought her paintings, it would be an outdoor scene, a red fox in the snow, geese flying overhead. An older woman, with a gleam of eccentricity, might buy one of her nudes. An older single man with money usually would pay quite a price, by Adirondack standards, for one of her nudes reclining with a tiger. That he would take back to the city with him. The scene of an Adirondack bog, near Nichols Pond, would hang on the stone chimney of his Adirondack camp, below the crossed snowshoes, and above the field stone mantelpiece, on which would sit carved shelf fungus, called artist's conk, and a family photo of his grandfather racing a rare wooden Idem sailboat on Upper St. Regis Lake.

This black fellow, Damian, would buy nothing, give her nothing but trouble, so of course, she gave in to Chantal.

"In the bunkhouse. If he stays, he stays in the bunkhouse. He can use the bathroom in the barn. I'll get Harry to check the plumbing. In the meantime, he can use the outhouse. But he has to work. If he's not a worker, he can't stay. His pay is room and board for the first month. After that we'll see."

"Thanks Mom," said Chantal, who crossed the room and hugged her, kissing Heidi on each cheek.

"Be careful of the brush. Be careful now, I'm not done." There was nothing that melted Heidi's heart more than being hugged by one of her daughters, each of whom she had dutifully breast-fed for six months back when they had nothing.

"I'm taking the truck. Be back later." Chantal looked at her watch. She'd be late for Damian, but, really, where's he going to go?

Heidi sighed and got up to stand back from her painting. She turned the painting upside down and walked back to their Ashley wood stove to look from there. "It's not balanced. It's out of whack, just like my daughter," she mumbled.

Jeff Kelly

Chantal was already past the prison, booming down the hill toward Port Henry and her Saturday night date. Boy, would there be talk. She popped in her Ninety-six Tears tape and felt young again.

twelve

Damian's only option for the night was to spend thirty-eight dollars to stay at the Champ Hotel behind the Grand Union. It sat high on the bluff above skin flats to the north and French settlement to the south, and had a breathtaking, panoramic view of the lake. Next to the billboard advertising the hotel was a big red sign with hand-painted white lettering listing the sightings of the Lake Champlain Monster called Champ. The small lobby where Damian signed in was really the vestibule of the owner's home. It was covered in glistening wainscoting from the floor to four feet up the wall, which was then plastered with drawings and newspaper articles and photos of persons like Joe Zarzynski in scuba gear in search of Champ. One prominently-displayed photo was framed and nailed to the wall next to a copy of a newspaper article displaying the same picture. The black and white photo was of a sea serpent in Bulwagga Bay which had sold to the New York Times for ten thousand dollars.

Damian's curiosity and ignorance of Port Henry and Champ overcame the proprietor's taciturn nature, and Pete explained as much as he could about the theory of Champ, how some people thought it was a large sturgeon fish, or the North American version of Loch Ness. Even though the number of sightings mirrored the rise and fall of local unemployment, Pete insisted there had been too many verified sightings for it to be nothing.

Along with Damian's room key, Pete, the proprietor, pointed to the telescope and told him he was welcome to use it. Damian had little to occupy his time except sleep and hope that Chantal pulled through for him. While there was still some light, he sat on the terrace outside his room in a red metal chair, touching it first to make sure it wasn't freshly painted, and then he gently rocked back to get the feel of the chair. He decided after his boot-camp incarceration, where every minute was accounted for, he liked having nothing to do. But in a few minutes he got up and sauntered back over to where he had signed in, and carefully took the telescope off the counter and walked back outside.

He had looked through a microscope but he had never looked through a telescope. Coming from the city, great distances didn't exist, unless he was on the top of a building and even then it had to be a tall building. Everything in the city was close-up. Astronomy wasn't possible, because you couldn't see the stars through the pollution and the glare and competition of the street lights. Maybe if he stood in the middle of 125th Street he could focus on something far away at the other end of the street. But of course he'd be run over. So this was his first time.

The telescope wasn't an old collapsible brass telescope, which might have been more in keeping with the historic nature of the town. Rather the eyepiece rotated among different powered lenses, and the silver telescope sat on a steel tripod. He chose a middle-range, 60x lens. It took him an eternity to get it focused. Finally in frustration, he swiveled the telescope south to his right, away from the expanse of water in front onto the span of the Crown Point Bridge, which was reflecting the evening sun.

Once focused he inched the field of vision from the deck to the pier to the abutment to the water. He began to get a feel for the knack of focusing and was drawn into the circular frame that enabled him to see like an owl. Underneath the bridge three kayakers paddled along. The lead green kayak made a left turn, and the others executed the same maneuver, but less crisply. Close to the three kayaks, a speed boat whisked by and the guy in the lead kayak paddled hard and surfed the wake while the other two bobbed and watched. Damian guessed that the paddler in the green kayak was a guide or was giving a lesson. Damian left the kayakers and followed along the wake until he picked up the speed boat.

The 21 Mine

While he was doing this Pete, the owner, sat down on the terrace with a Saranac beer in his hand.

Damian, his eye still pressed against the telescope, said. "Quite a sight."

"That's probably Spike's boat. It's past five, he gets home at four thirty and always hops into his Hacker Craft. I think he's got the only one on the Lake. You know him, Spike?"

Damian looked up at Pete quizzically. How was he supposed to know anybody around here.

"Spike Taylor. He works up at Moriah Shock. The big guy. He's one of the drill sergeants. I think they call him Hurricane."

"Oh, oh, yeah. Hurricane. He wasn't my C.O. Yeah, but I know who he is. Nice boat he's got."

As the boat moved north, its throaty sound filled the valley.

"Some of the environmentalists around here don't like that old boat, cause of the sound. But it can move, can't it? Of course you won't see Champ now, not with Taylor racing around."

Damian had forgotten that he was supposed to be searching for a sea monster.

"Champ's down at the bottom, now, four-hundred feet down. He'll come up again when it's darker."

Damian didn't know if he was serious or not. "How about that kayak guy, does he give lessons or anything?"

"Oh Jeff, yeah, right down there at Bulwagga Bay, He'll rent you a boat, life jacket, take you out, the whole nine yards. He's kind of a character though, full of wild ideas."

A whole new world opened up to Damian as he pressed his eye to the eyepiece wanting to see more. The possibilities thrilled him. He swiveled the telescope back out front to the great lake and scanned the dark surface, stopping to examine an errant wave, and then something floating in water. "I found something."

"Champ?" Pete asked with a twinkle.

"No," Damian said taking him seriously. "A long piece of wood with a number on it. Maybe a piece of a boat."

Pete knew his telescope was special, and all kinds of guests saw all kinds of things. He just helped them see what they wanted to see or were afraid of seeing.

"Here." Pete reached over and Damian pulled back from the eyepiece blinking. "Here. Let's use the highest power, 120x. But you got to have a surgeon's touch and you can't nudge the telescope."

While Pete made the adjustment, Damian surveyed the lake without the telescope but saw nothing. He waited anxiously to get back the telescope. Cautiously, Pete passed it over. First, Damian focused on a dock at the far shore of Vermont, four miles away. Once he was able to make out a ladder, leading from the dock up a rock cliff to a cabin, he returned to the water and crept back toward the spot where he had seen the floating wood. Patiently, he searched the blue and black wavy surface. His eye was tiring when he found the floating wooden remnant. It was curved, possibly a piece of the hull of a boat, and between splashes of waves a six digit number was visible.

Damian called out the numbers, "2 - 1 - 3 -." Suddenly, something broke the surface, something like a person's hand, up from the deep, scraped and bleeding, covering the last three numbers.

Damian twitched and froze. "I can't find it. I can't find it now." He had lost the powerful circle.

"Then it's gone," Pete said calmly. "It's always tricky with that lens. That's the Champ-sighting lens."

"2 - 1 - 3," Damian repeated. "Probably the beginning of a serial number."

Pete reached over to remove the telescope. Damian took his eye away from the telescope and bobbed back in his red chair, finally looking this concierge fellow Pete right in the eye. Damian didn't tell him about the hand. He tucked that away in a compartment of his mind. The whole thing was too peculiar, and he was starting to doubt himself.

One thing Damian was beginning to realize was that people who knew he was in prison, like this fellow Pete, and everyone else in Port Henry, were curious about him, in a respectful way, like they didn't want to offend him, like he might pull out a stiletto and stab them if they said the wrong thing. Little did they know that all he had done was smoke a bunch of pot. Well, sell a bunch of pot.

"So tell me about yourself," Pete said. "We don't get much of your kind up here."

Damian found himself actually using the training from Shock Incarceration, and waited to react. Was this guy being malicious thought Damian? No, he wasn't. So Damian took a long breath, picked up and slid the red chair on the concrete patio back between the two windows of his hotel room, so he could tilt the chair back against the wall. It was nice to have the time to bullshit after being in such a regimented environment for so long. Damian felt a surge of confidence.

"It all starts in Harlem, Pete. Do you mind if I call you Pete?"

"No, go right ahead. Here, have a beer," and Pete reached down into a brown bag and brought up another Saranac. He twisted the top off, put the cap in his shirt pocket, and handed it over to Damian.

Damian took a swig. He looked out at the last few reflected rays off the steel of the Crown Point bridge. He couldn't see the kayakers anymore, and the sounds of Taylor's boat were a distant rumbling. Damian leaned back and looked around, some of the tension easing out of him.

"I'm a free man," he said quietly. Even if this girl Chantal didn't pull through, he felt like he had made the right decision, not going back to his old neighborhood in the streets of Harlem. "Life is good."

"I'll drink to that," Pete said.

They heard sirens in the background, but Pete didn't seem to think it was a big deal. "Probably someone had a heart attack. Nowadays, someone gets a stomach ache and they send out an ambulance and two fire trucks."

"Anyway, my dad's name is Reggie and my mom's is Betty. He has one foot in the white world that makes money, an advertising agency, and one foot in the black world that knows how to spend it and have fun. But that's part of the problem. After he got successful, making a lot of dough, he started dating other women." Damian frowned. "Particularly this white woman at work."

Pete could tell he didn't want to dwell on that.

Quickly, Damian shoved up the sleeve on his left arm to show Pete his Mom's name tattooed above a heart on his shoulder. "She was really a looker in her day. When she dresses up to go to church, she can still turn a few heads. My

Ma's pretty angry about the whole thing - me going away for selling a harmless drug like pot; all the musicians use it."

"My dad used to play the saxophone. Said he wasn't any good. But sometime on a Sunday evening, when he was home, and things were good between he and Ma, he'd play out on the stoop in the late afternoon, especially if it was hot. And we'd all hang with him waiting on the neighbors and street hawkers, to drift by, which they always did. 'All right Reggie, all right Reggie,' they would say.

"Anyway, so I don't hate crackers. My dad works in the white world. And I know both, and I can tolerate both. There's good and bad everywhere." As Damian talked his eyes were fixated on the lake. "I was always good in school. It just came naturally to me, so ma and dad were real proud of me, except for now.

"They're saying it's because I got hooked up with the wrong crowd, especially this guy Laverne, who was older and lived by himself. They blame it on him - a bad apple. My dad said if he ever comes around again, he'll shoot him. But he won't have to. He's Upstate too, in Dannemora doing ten years for armed robbery. I never knew there were so many prisons up here." Damian clunked down forward on his chair.

"But I'm looking to the future. Do you know the Beauvais clan, Heidi the rancher and her daughters?" Damian asked.

"Sure, we all know them, at least who they are. She's quite a painter, you know."

"Yeah, her daughter, Chantal, told me her mom paints animals and nudes. Chantal modeled for her Mom once. She's in a picture with a tiger. I haven't seen it yet."

"I bet you want to see it," Pete chuckled.

"I want to see the real thing," Damian grinned. "I'm supposed to meet her tomorrow in front of the Chinese Restaurant." Then to himself more than to Pete, he said the word "Saturday" like it was precious word. Something he might have dreamed about on the inside. Damian smiled sweetly. "Yeah, I have a date."

"Lucky you. Here, have another beer." Pete pulled another one of those Saranac's out of his bag. They drank and talked on into the night, and then the phone rang.

The 21 Mine

"I'd better get that," Pete said. He got up while Damian enjoyed the view of the bridge lights twinkling in the dark.

Pete returned immediately. "You must bring excitement with you. You're done right? You're properly released?"

"Oh yeah, I graduated. One of the prison guards, Billy, even waved to me in town."

"Well, they got the road blocked. There's a guard on the hill with a shotgun stopping cars. Somebody's escaped. I said this would happen."

"Holy Shit." Damian leaned forward, shaking his head from side to side. "I wonder if I know him?"

Jeff Kelly

thirteen

Just when the parties of the New York State Department of Correctional Services, the New York State Department of Environmental Conservation, the New York State Troopers and the Essex County Sheriff's Department had agreed, after tortuous all night negotiations, that Warden DeJesus would be in charge of the search party, a maroon Astroliner roared up along the sandy ATV road, a handicapped symbol on the license plate and Nature Conservancy stickers on the tinted windows, skidding sideways to a stop.

"Goddamn it," the Warden seethed. "Not more of this jurisdictional crap!"

"On no," moaned Spike, placing his rifle down after having meticulously adjusted the scope. "The holy Adirondack Conservancy. They're worse than the A.P.A."

Ring, who was the head of the DEC, knew the head of the Conservancy from skiing and clinking glasses at fund raisers. Ring handed his briefcase to his own assistant and walked over to the space age van as an electric motor whirred. The sliding doors opened and a projecting steel arm extended, lowering an attached metal platform onto the ground, bearing a smiling Tommy Arnet, like the lead actor making his entrance on a thrust stage.

K-9 Officer Frank LaPointe from Ticonderoga grabbed the leash, just in time, as his police dog Fury lunged at the contraption and its human cargo.

"Welcome," Ring called out as he walked over.

"I heard you were here," Tommy called back as he shifted his twenty thousand dollar, off-road, motorized wheelchair and buzzed off the platform directly toward Ring into the midst of the bureaucrats, some in uniform, others in blue jeans and wool shirts.

Sheriff's deputies, two town cops, a couple of firemen, rock climbers from the Keene Backcountry Rescue Unit with an abundance of ropes and climbing gear, and at least a dozen armed guards, including Billy with a shot gun, plus a phalanx of troopers and forest rangers, all cast their eyes at the latest arrival to whom the other bureaucratic bigwigs all appeared to kowtow. Following the lead of the DEC's Ring, a parade of agency officials felt compelled to file before Tommy.

"Greetings," Tommy said with a touch of irony. "My wife was stopped by a guard with a shot gun last night on Route 9N. She was on her way home to Westport after picking up Chinese in Port Henry, and because of you guys, she was late and my moo goo gai pan was cold."

Tommy was a pro at putting people at ease.

The sun was reflecting off Tommy's suntanned head. In his day Tommy would have been doing the rappelling himself, so he got his due respect and more so because he always smiled and never complained about his condition. About two years ago in the Adirondack backcountry a wall of ice gave way on a first ascent. Tom fell forty feet and broke his spinal cord.

"Ring," Tommy said, as he used his finger to call him over, "come here. Now this is no shit. Those mines are full of Indiana bats and they're an endangered species. Now your agency gave us jurisdiction over verifying and tabulating their existence here. They do exist. This is the only site east of the Mississippi, and I don't want them harmed."

"Neither do I," Ring said calmly.

"Before the accident," he said forthrightly, patting his chair, "Kelly and I - you know, that crazy editor of Adirondack Life, and your guy Hicks, went down there and counted them."

"You went down into the 21 Mine?" Ring questioned incredulously.

The 21 Mine

Lowering his voice, Tommy said, "Well not those exact mines, but the ones on Fisher Hill back beneath the prison. So I want assurances that the habitat of the Indiana bats won't be disturbed."

At that point the warden, who had been listening, walked over and introduced himself, feeling that this was a problem he could handle. "Billy, come here. Would you assure Mr. Arnet that no bats will be disturbed." In a gracious tone the Warden, who could give a hoot about saving bats or their habitat, said to Tommy, "Billy is going down in there as my personal representative, and I will add that to his list of instructions."

Tommy asked the warden for his card, and turned to his aide who inserted it in a manila folder tucked under his arm. Of course, like everyone else, Tommy was here for the excitement too. Even with all the prisons popping up in the Adirondacks like mushrooms, it wasn't very often they had a genuine break-out.

For a minute the Warden hesitated, but then he realized the Indiana bat issue had been handled and Tommy was staying here for the show. The Warden relaxed, and adjusted his tie.

The first streaks of daylight illuminated the encamped gathering and everybody took their turns looking down beyond the edge, marveling at the vast 21 pit, checking out what they were up against.

"So who's the nut case?" Tommy asked the warden as they watched the backcountry unit secure safety ropes in preparation for beginning the descent.

"His name is Wallace Klocks and he's dangerous. He shouldn't have been in here in the first place. He's not like the other inmates."

"How so?" Tommy asked, just making conversation, his energy beginning to fade.

The Warden looked around for reporters before he responded. "He's hard core," he whispered, as if that information were classified.

Tommy had undergone a monumental struggle to retain the movement of his arms and torso. Depending on his cocktail of medications, he tired easily. Tommy motioned to his cross-country skiing buddy Ring to help his aide lift him into some shade back from the cliff. If Tom stayed where he was and pressed the wrong button, his Hummer-like wheelchair might surge over the edge.

After he was properly positioned under a leafy sumac tree, Tommy surveyed the drop beyond the lip of the gigantic crater that contained a marvel of tunnels. The cooler night air at the bottom of canyon was colliding with the warming air of a sunny morning, and the plumes of mist set Tommy to dreaming of a time high up the wind-blown face of Mt. Marcy. He and the Ski-To-Die gang had dropped off the top cornice, causing a small avalanche, yet still managing to ski upright and traverse the crusty bowl. That had been a rush. He took a measure of pleasure in the fact, that in his day, he had done those things, used his legs and body to experience outdoor, athletic excitement. Now all he could do was watch, and occasionally reminisce to good friends, careful to avoid the maudlin. He dared not think like this too often, fearful that dwelling on the past might bring on depression.

With concentrated effort he put on his Yankees cap to protect his shiny bald head from the rising sun. In a strained voice, Tommy yelled to the rock climber in the second team, whom he had rappelled with in his glory days, "Indiana bats have small ears and twelve inch wing spans."

The day was warming up and the clouds of thick mist were drifting higher. This 21 Mine phenomenon heightened the perils and swathed searchers and onlookers in obscuring fog.

Three teams of four began the descent. Each consisted of a forest ranger, a rock climber with a rope, a guard with a rifle, and an Emergency Medical Technician (EMT) with a portable radio. One roped-in team was wearing orange backpacks supplied by the local outfitter, the Mountaineer. Unknowingly they were scrambling down the exact moonlit route Klocks took. The other teams were rappelling over a steeper rock face, belaying each other in sections.

For the next twenty minutes, Warden DeJesus, Ring of the DEC, detectives from the Westport trooper barracks, and a host of other men participating in a manly activity at dawn in the mountains, were silent and motionless except to sip their black coffee and turn their wrists to look at their Swiss Army watches. They realized, with the emphasis on safety and proper procedure, these guys would be gone for a while. The Moriah fire departments from Mineville and Witherbee were hauling in portable generators and lights in preparation for lighting the rim of the canyon throughout the night.

The 21 Mine

Warden A.D. broke the silence to pontificate a bit. "Prisoners think and talk about escaping just the way lottery players think and talk about winning the big one. 'Let's see, when I win, should I take my money in annual payments or one lump sum?' But few win the lottery and few escape and if they do, they are usually captured . . . dead," A.D. said smugly trying to disguise his concern.

"Cons watch movies about prison escapes and know the only way to get the dogs off their scent is to go to the water. " The Warden stopped to look around, wishing he had a chair to tilt back in, knowing that he was entertaining the troops, so to speak. He finished with a sneer and commented, "One problem is most prisoners can't swim. So we usually find them drowned."

"Thing about water," he continued, "water is an earthly substance which moves on its own; always falling from the sky in the form of rain or snow, always flowing downward in the form of a brook or river; always filling up mining shafts cut and carved out of rock and stone."

Just when the Warden and the pack of officials were relaxed from bullshitting, yet itchy from standing around, the local press showed. Susie from The Valley News pulled up in her rust-covered Volvo, camera in hand, her youngest asleep in the car seat in the back.

"Hi guys, what's up? " she beamed. Of course everyone knew what was up, and even she knew what was up. She was just saying hi. She was young, in her twenties, an over-educated import from Princeton, who was well liked in spite of her background and liberal tilt. Her ebullient nature eventually won most everybody over along with her looks. Not drop-dead good looking, but pretty with a nice body that she did her best to disguise with baggy gray sweaters and blue jean jackets.

The men deferred to Warden DeJesus, who hiked one foot up on a stump, wiping flecks of dirt off the shiny black tip of his shoe. He was probably one of the few officials who didn't know her. The paper didn't cover the prisons - except when something like this happened.

A genuine prison break, Susie couldn't believe it. She was so excited she even paid to get a sitter to take care of her other two kids. Her carpenter husband would be pissed about the piles of dirty laundry that she wouldn't get to, but too bad.

The Warden and Susie exchanged pleasantries, and then Susie slipped into her reporter mode and asked the who, what, when, where and why. The Warden emphasized that since Moriah Shock was a minimum security and most prisoners had to volunteer to have their sentences reduced and then in turn qualify, there weren't even bars on the windows except for a couple of cells for recalcitrant inmates, most of whom would be shipped back to where they came from.

"Was this Klocks guy in one of those cells?" she asked.

"Yes he was."

"Was he due to be shipped out?"

The Warden hesitated, and gently, with his hand on her elbow, steered her away from the other officials, especially the state police and administrative personnel from the Correctional Services.

"Actually, we had planned to hold him there until his time was up."

"When was that?"

"In twenty-three days he was eligible for parole," the Warden said waiting for the inevitable surprise.

"Wow, less than a month," Susie repeated. "That's strange. Why on earth would anyone try to escape with a few weeks left?" Warden DeJesus failed to mention that Klocks was scheduled to testify in ten days in a smuggling case in federal court in Albany.

"That's a good question. Plus look where he has escaped to. A bottomless pit."

They both stared out into the misty sky over the crater rim.

The Warden was trying to float the idea that maybe Klocks was trying to commit suicide. Maybe he was mentally unbalanced.

"Do you think you'll find him?"

"Alive? No."

fourteen

Klocks found his own footprints, some clearly imprinted in the ice and mud, the others washed away in a stream. He made his way to the largest of the three openings, feeling the chill from the drop in temperature as the mass of the cold pre-dawn air fell to the floor of the canyon, mixing with the constant fifty-two degrees of the mines.

A crack, and then a plunging sound like a wall of scaffolding collapsing sent Klocks cringing in a ball as one of the tooth-like icicles dropped and exploded on impact, sending chunks of ice flying. He rose shaken and realized that his potential savior, the 21 Mine, was also his most potent enemy. If nature was a God, down here it was a fickle God.

Another thunderous clatter echoed up from some underground chamber, a hunk of ice or iron ore, loosened by the collapsed icicle, ricocheting off the walls of a shaft as it went down, down, down. Finally, there was silence.

He took a last look skyward. A crooked row of lights flickered at the canyon rim. A larger light, some sort of portable searchlight swept down his route. But no light could reach as far as he had come.

Though he felt little pain, his foot continued to bleed from his fall onto the glacier. He walked into the mine entrance until he could no longer see the gathering lights of his distant followers. The cavernous entrance was larger than his neighborhood Troy Bank building. He unzipped the bag's side pocket and took out his flashlight. It was dry and still worked. Klocks was standing on a thin, watery layer of melting snow flowing over ice. He knelt down to untie his boot, take off his sock, and examine his wound. A gash, but not too bad. He stuffed his prison-issue sock; bloody, muddy and wet, into the boot.

He removed his New Balance running shoes from the bag, took off his other boot, and used the cleaner white sock as a tourniquet over the gash on his other ankle. He put the size ten Ds running shoes on, and walked over the slippery ice, leaving no footprints.

He stopped and thought for a moment. This was no good. He walked back the three meters to where he had laid his boots next to swirls of blood. He picked up the bloodless boot and carried it with him to the rear of the cavern. He held his flashlight in one hand and got down and crept on all fours toward a cold, black shaft. With his bare hand, he felt for dry rock and found a higher ridge. He reached down to his wound, and with his fingers smeared some blood on the dry rock. He tossed his good boot down the shaft, and listened in silence until seconds later he heard a faint splashing sound.

He retraced his footsteps in the flowing water, and grabbed the other bloodied boot. As he approached the outside opening of the cavern, he switched off his flashlight, and then reconsidered. He gazed upwards and saw rows of lights, more than before - the encampment of an invading army.

Pressing with his thumb, he turned on his flashlight, aware the searchers might see the beam, and scanned the glacier and snow for the footprints he had made. When the prints disappeared on the watery ice, he pressed off the light and with an underhand motion as if he were pitching horseshoes, tossed his boot and bloody sock at the last footprint.

Now his decoys were set, his feint was complete. He had set a trail into the mine opening, into the slippery blackness, to the edge of a perilous shaft. He pondered his route in the opposite direction. Before sunrise he had to make it to the higher pillared mines, the ones with the beckoning eyes. And leave no trace on the way. "No trace," he whispered.

A physical challenge lay ahead of him. Another collapsing sound from the back of the cavern startled him. He made sure everything on him was attached; that there was nothing to drop. He let his own feral nature take over, leaving no prints, treading only on the watery ice with his waffle-soled running shoes, walking up and into one of the many rivulets. He doubted the dogs could get down here, but if they did, they should lose his scent in the water.

Klocks drew strength from his boyhood nickname, "The Owl." His cronies used to call him that in South Troy. When the cops were chasing him he would use his remarkable climbing ability to scale a building or climb a tree and watch his pursuers beneath him as they hunted for him. Recalling his past, he cooed out loud, "I am the Owl."

He was having difficulty transforming the eyes of the tunnels he was climbing toward into any kind of safe symbol, but he dare not stop. Exhaustion coupled with a glimmer of daylight propelled him forward.

His pounding chest reminded him of one time in Troy, when he had escaped the cops by running up fourteen flights of stairs, beating the elevator, and gaining access to the roof. When the cops arrived on the elevator they started down the stairwell, sure that they had him trapped.

The rush of the water covered the sounds of the rocks and stones he sent tumbling and sliding. Far above on the canyon rim, the searchlight was off. The guards probably had sent out for Dunkin Donuts. That's when SWAT teams made mistakes. They waited too long, until they were coordinated with other agencies, bulletproof-vested, mentally prepared, and fed. Two young, determined guards trained as rock climbers could have caught him, but now with every breath, with every handhold, Klocks was closer to his hideout.

Nearby, something fluttered. A bat was returning to the same anthropomorphic mines Klocks was climbing toward. Even the bats avoided the cold watery shafts below. Within a few minutes, a cloud of bats was flying about him, homing in on the pillared caves. A ray of light seared the gray sky. Like a vampire bat, who must get to his roost before dawn, Klocks scrambled up to the higher mines, frantic to get to his own crypt.

A second stream of light shot out over the canyon rim. If somebody spotted him now, his plan would be destroyed. He reached up to a piece of wood holding back detritus. It was a twenty feet section of a wooden ladder, decayed, but somehow still set in the eroding, rocky hillside. Next to it a cable dangled directly out of one of the tunnels. Petrified of the coming daylight, he took a chance and lunged, grabbing the cable end with both hands, rappelling off the crumbling rock. With his waning strength he shinnied up into the mine opening. As the bats whirred overhead, baseball-size chunks of ore ricocheted off the rocks below. He scrambled inside, relieved to be hidden by the blackness and collapsed on a dry ledge.

* * * *

If it weren't for the frigid winters, Klocks might have settled in the Adirondacks. He liked the frontier atmosphere and lack of local cops. Stay off the Northway and you could pretty much do as you please. Especially a skillful con-artist like Klocks.

Klocks was forty-two with a fairly lengthy felony record, albeit no violence with a gun. He felt guns made punks, who were basically spineless creatures, into bullies. Mano a mano, that's the way Klocks liked it. Klocks was always the exception. His incarceration had nothing to do with drugs. He saw drugs as weakness, and felt superior to any man who used or sold drugs. And, unlike most prisoners, Klocks didn't confide in others except to falsely draw them into his confidence. He seldom let his true thoughts be known. None of the other prisoners comprehended how cold and ingenious Klocks could be. They thought he was just a thief, a rather crafty one who specialized in antiques and paintings. He was that and more.

When his transfer papers and records came through to Moriah Shock, both Warden A.D. and Thomason, the prison counselor, thought Klocks was a mistake. The Warden phoned Albany and discovered that Klocks' case had been handled outside the normal channels, by the Detective Syndicate. With a raised eyebrow and a good deal of reluctance the Warden signed the acceptance papers.

Mercurial and mean, Klocks was a determined physical specimen, and a professional crook. "A thief," is how he proudly referred to himself, "in the tradition of Robin Hood," he would sometimes add with a chuckle. He grew up poor and lower class on First Avenue in South Troy. Being a crook was his job, his life. Klocks worked all the angles of his profession, doing whatever it took to gain an advantage for himself, which is why he was here in minimum, and the other guy, who had the misfortune of doing a job with Klocks, got life.

The 21 Mine

Early in his career as a thief, Klocks visited the Shellburne Museum in Vermont, and stole an original volume of lithographs of John James Audubon's "The Birds of America." Since Klocks' boyhood nickname was Owl, when he came upon the page on the Great Horned Owl, with its sharp talons and hooked bill, he tore it out and carried the crumpled page around until he had memorized and in some cases assimilated the traits of America's largest and most powerful owl. He practiced turning his head like the owl, but could only manage 180 degrees, not the 270 degrees of which the owl was capable. Klocks' ears were even slightly asymmetrical like that of the owl. He learned that sound, not sight, was the owl's keenest sense, and he incorporated that knowledge into his own body and soul.

He was caught selling the original Audubon volume to an antiquarian bookstore in Saratoga Springs, called the Lyrical Ballad. Eight months later, he was convicted and given a fairly lengthy, three year sentence, in part because of the Museum's fury over the one missing page on the owl. He ended up serving 27 months.

That theft and the stealing of an original Winslow Homer drawing from a summer home on the North Shore in Westport in Essex County, established Klocks' credentials as a self-taught art and antiques thief, who could tell the real thing from a reproduction. At an exclusive, second floor art dealer on Madison and 68th in New York City, where you had to be buzzed up, he received twenty-seven thousand dollars - and no questions asked - for the Winslow Homer drawing.

The following summer, after the Wesport family saw the drawing listed in a catalogue promoting an upcoming Sotheby's auction, the family was forced to buy it back because they had no papers proving they were part of the painting's provenance. They did however arrange to pay for its repurchase, prior to the auction to the public, with money they had collected from insurance covering the theft of the original drawing. Little did the prominent Westport family realize that the person who stole the drawing, which may well have been a sketch for Homer's painting "A Basket of Clams," was now housed in a minimum security prison in the neighboring town of Moriah.

Klocks also lifted a cast-iron penny bank from the same camp in Westport, but the owners never reported that loss. It was an early American William Tell penny bank which generally went at auctions for about eighteen hundred dollars. If you pressed the archer's foot, he shot a penny, which knocked off the apple on the way to clanking into a slot in a turret. Klocks suspected the owners, who were elderly, didn't know it was missing.

He stole it from a back shelf in the pantry the same wintry day he snatched the Winslow Homer drawing off the cluttered dining room wall. The temperature inside the Great Camp was four below zero. Two days and two hundred miles later, on the other side of the Adirondacks, he sold the bank to a pawn shop in Rochester for four hundred dollars.

A Moriah Shock van routinely passed the driveway to that summer house, a Great Camp, where Klocks had stolen the painting and the bank. A windy, uphill driveway led to the stone and pine log building among virgin pines with a view of the lake. Klocks always took a window seat on the van, glimpsed the tops of the stone chimneys and gave a knowing wink.

The van's destination was Twin Valleys, in the woods between Lewis and Wadhams. There the inmates, wearing red wool toques and green jackets, selectively logged the woods using two man bucksaws. The whole scene of sawing, splitting and stacking wood against the white snow and brown cabins was quite picturesque, almost Christmasy. Mornings were cold and the army-green, stitched, down jackets the inmates wore, looking like they were made in China, were actually made right here at home, farther north in Ray Brook at Camp Gabriels, another of the many Adirondack prisons.

One time earlier in the winter they bypassed Twin Valleys and drove an hour north to Saranac Lake to help the inmates from Camp Gabriels finish this ice palace in time for a winter festival. They sawed blocks of ice from the lake and carted them to a parking lot where they built a full scale, glittering, ice-blue palace complete with towers and circular turrets. Photographers from the Daily Enterprise and Adirondack Life took pictures of the inmates thirty feet up, lifting the top blocks in place. At the end of the day the guards from Camp Gabriels bought pizza, and inmates and guards stood side by side eating slices, bedazzled by what they had created.

fifteen

After a deep nap of unknown duration on his rocky perch, Klocks awoke cold and sore. His whole body ached, and he reached down to his ankle and felt crusted blood. He moaned. Water dripped near him, and he palmed a few drops, licking them from his hand.

Gradually, his state of alertness rose until the noise of a small rock slide, mostly skittering scree, caught his attention. His ability to visualize   kicked in and he knew they were coming down the sides of crater, looking for him, sending small stones sliding before them, like droplets before a thunderstorm.

From the breast pocket of his denim shirt, he pulled out the folded map he had made from memory. At the prison library he had studied the historical drawings of the side tunnels leading from the 21 Mine, which on that map was labeled the 'Bonanza 21' mine. His hand drawn map was wet but readable and showed that a drift labeled the Welch tunnel once led horizontally away from the 21 pit. Its location was somewhere near the last unexploded twenty thousand ton pillar of iron ore which stood like a sphinx just fifteen feet from where he lay.

With effort and stealth he crept off his rock perch, across the cave floor next to the pillar, avoiding the puddles and piles of bat guano. Behind a slab of rock that had fallen from the top of the one hundred and twenty foot, iron-rich pillar, he peered out across the crater.

He watched the progress of the search parties with a sense of aloofness. They were tiny figures, far away, with splotches of orange on their backs. He caught the reflective glint from the barrel of a rifle, and that angered him. Bringing weapons angered him. Yes, he was a killer, but they didn't know that. Only his victims knew it, and they were all petty criminals, who deserved what they got - and Klocks never used a gun. They had messed with the wrong guy, that's all. Klocks chuckled out loud. He liked that thought. They didn't know who they were messing with. Programmed robots who couldn't behave and breathe like an animal, the way he could. Hidden in his aerie, he glowered at his predators, who were now below his level on the other side of the vast pit, descending to the mammoth tunnels at the bottom of the 21 Mine.

"Been there, done that," he said as he receded back from the edge. He cupped another drink of water and crawled back to the ledge. Back to the lair he had come from.

Two bats fluttered in from the outside sunlight, stragglers from their nightly hunt for insects. Bats didn't bother Klocks. He was accustomed to them. As a kid in Troy, he had encountered bats while exploring the caves of the Poestenkill River. He followed the erratic flight of the pair until they disappeared in the darkness in the upper corner of the mine. That's where he would start.

From his Nike bag he unscrewed his jar of peanut butter and with two fingers scooped out his breakfast, and then screwed the top back on. Discipline. He had been fed well at prison, so he was prepared for some deprivation. That and another gulp of water was his breakfast. No problem. He could live off one meal for a week. After all, the more you eat, the more you shit. He removed a candle and matches from his bag. He scoured the area to eliminate any possible traces of a human. No shoe prints in the sand, nothing.

He began to move farther into the blackness of his tunnel, but stopped. He needed a stick to detect the hazardous shafts, to feel ahead. He thought of the disintegrating ladder that was still attached to the cliff outside.

Back he crawled to the corner of the lip where he had come up. His pursuers were well below him. Two of the three search teams had traversed down the steeper sections, and were now clustered together, some on their knees, examining the ice and dirt next to a silt-laden stream.

That's good, Klocks thought. They've probably found my blood-soaked sock, more proof that I ventured into the flooded mines below. The pumps had

The 21 Mine

been turned off since 1987, and if the engineer's calculations were correct, in about 10 years, right about now, most of the mines would be flooded to within five hundred feet of the surface, or roughly just below the entrances to the mines at the bottom of this 21 crater.

Klocks heard it before he saw it. A pulsating thump-thump coming from somewhere over the horizon of the 21 pit. He immediately pulled back into the safety of his mine entrance, just like the fledging ravens who pulled back into their nests one rock ledge above Klocks.

The searchers below knew this bird was coming. They looked up at the arrival of a state police helicopter from the Westport trooper barracks. The Warden's plan, in consultation with the state police, was for the helicopter to hover down into the 21 pit while the copilot scanned the tunnel and cave entrances in search of a live Klocks or a dead body. The thinking was the helicopter might save the searchers from the dangerous task of exploring the depths of the 21 pit.

Instead, the dust, dirt, silt and snow, which was two or three feet deep toward the bottom third of the canyon, was stirred up, and a ferocious cloud of particles rose up making visibility impossible, endangering the stability of the helicopter. As the pilot fought to get the helicopter the hell our of there, its blades nearly swiped the pillar next to where Klocks was hiding. The disoriented, wind-blown searchers rubbed bits of iron ore dust from their eyes.

Klocks realized ego was what did in most criminals, yet he was not immune from taking similar risks. The idiocy of returning to the scene of the crime. The stupid criminals, which most were, and even the bright, determined ones, like Klocks, enjoyed their reputations in the underworld of crime. His favorite song was Hammer's "You Can't Touch That," which to Klocks meant, you can't touch me.

Mumbling that bit of bravado, Klocks flattened himself on chiseled rock, still in the shadows, and reached over the edge with one arm, grabbing the rotten top rung of the ladder. It had been bolted there to the rock since the miners had reclaimed the ore from other pillars in explosions sixty years ago. He twisted it in his hand and jerked upward, tempting fate with the noise of an errant rock which might alert the searchers to look up. Klocks came away with a three foot long splinter to use as a poker and a staff. It would have to do as his third eye, as he tried to squirm and crawl his way through his own coffin-like tunnel.

The searchers were entering the caverns below when a giant whoosh and rumble shook the entire canyon. Water from one shaft must have broken through, and was now cascading down a tunnel with God-awful power, like the charge from a broken dam. Periodically, the dormant mines belched like some sort of subterranean, living organism. Klocks stood up, out of sight, and gawked at this beast of a pit, known as the 21 Mine. The passage behind him might lead to his grave or to another world. Candle in hand, he walked into the blackness, just like he planned.

Klocks headed back toward the upper corner the bats had fluttered to. The ceiling and floor funneled together, so that now he could touch the dripping rock near his head, while crunching on crushed stone. He took a last look at the blinding oval of light behind him, thinking the searchers down below were doing the same thing he was, seeking a way out, or an answer to their task. If they found his body, their task was finished. If they found his bloody shoe and sock where he had tossed them, and then spots of blood near the edge of a black, bottomless shaft, that might be enough, eventually, to call off the search.

That he would be presumed dead, is what Klocks was counting on. Klocks was looking for a new start, a new identity and a final way out. He was sick of cooperating with the police, sick of conning them, sick of playing the game, yet determined to be the winner. If he could physically tunnel out of his perch, and escape, really escape into a new reality . . .

Wallace Klocks had read the history of mining in Moriah, and he was determined to make that knowledge work for him. He was sure that he could find another way out of the 21 Mine, either north through Welch and then to Lover's Hole or simply through some forgotten tunnel beyond the perimeter lip of the 21, Bonanza-Joker Bed.

The two key shafts which led into this rich vein were called Joker and Bonanza. The 21 Mine encompassed them both and was named after the lucky gambling number. The mining complex was called by a mixture of those names, with '21' and '21 Bonanza' being the most popular. Klocks preferred the '21 Joker' tag, hoping it would bring him good luck.

The 21 Mine

Klocks used one wooden match to light the candle, making sure he stuffed the match into the pocket of his prison overalls. The fact that this passageway was slanting slightly upward was a positive one for him. He wanted to get to burial depth, so he could poke his head up through the earth's crust and rise up like the living dead.

Get on with it, he said to himself. For some reason he was delaying. The air was still. The sides were closing in on him. He was forced to stoop as he crept farther into this rock crevasse. No bats were on the sides, no dung was on the floor. He took that as a bad sign, since bats were a sign of life. He turned sideways as the walls pressed in. He reached out with his stick and tapped a hard, chipped-out wall ahead of him. The opening narrowed to nothing. He felt no breeze. He had come maybe forty feet to a dead end. He backed out, discouraged but not despondent. It just meant one dead end he could eliminate. A no that made him one step closer to a yes. When there was enough room to turn around, he saw the oval of sunlight. He was back to where he started.

Klocks tightened his stomach muscles, took a deep breath to settle himself and blew out the candle. Twice a bat dived near his head, and then flew up and disappeared behind another large rubble of rocks. Klocks picked up one of the softball-size rocks, rich in iron ore and magnesium. It was impressively heavy, and glittered. One side of the six-sided rock was cylindrical and smooth, drilled out for inserting dynamite. Klocks contemplated the chunk in his hand, felt the weight, and concluded he could kill a man with one blow.

The black chunk of iron ore which Klocks held in his hand was typical of the 21-Joker Mine. It was a mass of crystals of pure magnetite, the richest iron ore ever found in the United States. Another shaft farther north in the Barton Hill Mine, where these nodules of sparkling iron were found was called Lover's Hole. It's only known entrance was through a four thousand foot shaft. The 21 Mine complex was full of forgotten and uncharted tunnels which had not been sealed off. All Klocks needed to do was to find one that led north away from the 21 Mine to a distant light hole.

Klocks dropped the chunk of ore at the base of the pile, as a bat flew out over his head toward the sunlight and then back to the top of the broken and blasted rock.

Klocks thought for a moment, and then carefully on all fours, climbed the dusty rubble, until he was on top, still a hundred feet below the cavern ceiling. He felt a slight breeze, which encouraged him. He was stepping away from the twilight zone and into the darkness again. He found a hole in the cavern wall behind the rubble. An endangered Indiana bat was fluttering in and out of a jagged hole. Klocks knew that was where he had to go.

sixteen

Weary and wet, the searchers described the scene at the bottom of the 21 pit as something out of the movie Indiana Jones. They radioed for more cave lights to be sent down. One trooper called the scene "dark, dangerous and slippery." A maze of side tunnels and vertical shafts surrounded the three main mine entrances of Clonan, Bonanza and Joker. The searchers had the boot and they found Klocks' footprints and spots of blood leading to the edge of a shaft.

Each team explored one of the tunnels with the warning from DeJesus not to take any unnecessary risks. "We don't want a second death on our hands," DeJesus stated. As the hours clicked by, and there was no answer to their shouts which echoed every which way down the tunnels, and Wallace Klocks wasn't found, the assumption among the searchers, first articulated to the press by the Warden, was that Klocks had fallen down a mine shaft and drowned.

Late Sunday night, really early Monday morning, at the end of fifty-four hours of searching, Warden DeJesus called for a gathering of the heads of each organization to meet behind the hot dog stand at 5:00 a.m. Billy was instructed to keep the press away with the promise of an announcement at 6:00 a.m.

In the meantime, Tommy Arnet, had left and returned. He was ever trying to win people over, and told Jessie, who ran the concession truck, to offer free doughnuts and coffee during the meeting courtesy of the Adirondack

Conservancy. This led to a kind of festival atmosphere among the searchers, onlookers and reporters.

During the meeting, the department heads stood with their arms crossed, holding their coffee next to their biceps. Tommy maneuvered his Hummer on the highest ground just outside the circle of active participants, but within hearing distance. In the back of a trooper's car on a white towel lay a bloody sock and one prison issue Riddell boot. Next to it were photos of the boot print down in the pit. They matched. The department heads agreed that the escapee, as they referred to him, had raced down the 21 pit and disappeared into one of the mines at the bottom.

On a dirt road between Moriah Shock and the 21 pit, three dogs, two of them tied to trailers, had barked the night Klocks ran by. A Mineville woman in a white frame house, sipping her hot toddy, and rocking to the erratic rhythm of Rush Limbaugh on the radio, had told the detectives that the prisoner ran right down the road, and her part-shepherd dog Francie, chased after him.

On the other side of the Lincoln Pond Road, Klocks had trampled the blueberry bushes before he got onto the path of the four wheelers winding through the fields. It was clear by the broken limbs of the birch entwined in the mesh fence, where he had scrambled over, choosing a spot where the tree had grown into the barb wire, enabling him to grab hold and vault down to the ground.

"It's almost like the guy is not thinking right," Ring said.

"Most crooks don't," said one of the detectives from the trooper barracks.

"But, he made no effort to hide his tracks," Ring said.

"No question, he's just running," a sheriff's deputy said.

"Why though, why would anyone escape with one month to serve? That's crazy," Billy said shaking his head in disbelief.

"Yes," DeJesus said, swatting some flecks of grass off the crease of his right pant leg, "And why run down into that godforsaken pit, when there's no way out?"

"Bats go in and out and so did I," Tommy said weakly from behind the tight circle of men. With his good right hand he powered his wheelchair closer. Tommy was adept at one-liners, which is why he thrived at cocktail parties.

The 21 Mine

"But let's keep in mind, he can't fly," remarked one of the unidentified state agency men.

"I had on climbing boots and a miner's head lamp and I almost slipped down one of those shafts. Without a rope . . . I think he's no longer with us," concluded one of the Keene climbers.

"Fifty-two degrees gentlemen, fifty-two degrees. I could last in those temperatures if I stayed dry and calm." As an afterthought, Tommy added, "You couldn't be afraid of the dark, though, or bats."

"Tommy, enough with the bats, will ya," Ring said as he took his pipe out of his mesh pocket, happy to have the chance to wear the fly-fishing vest on the job, and started the ritual of lighting his pipe.

"Another issue," chimed in the sheriff, who weighed three hundred and ten pounds and wore a white Stetson cowboy hat. "We're using taxpayers' money to find a criminal who has nothing to do with us here in Essex County. I say erect an electric fence around the perimeter of this crazy canyon, and if he manages to crawl out of his tomb, he'll get fried."

DeJesus consulted his watch and glanced at Billy. "We've been at this for more than 48 hours. Resources do cost money. We've got to start to thinking about overtime." He looked around, trying to gauge what the other agency heads really thought. Most of them we're looking tired. Plus tomorrow, rather today, was Monday, and these guys were all accountable to nine to five jobs, though only a few would report to them. No one, except maybe the spelunkers, would want to continue rappelling into mining shafts.

The only man DeJesus was wary of was the state official from the Detective Syndicate who had flashed a whole wallet full of credentials. DeJesus, who was suspicious, called his Albany office to have him checked out. DeJesus thought this skinny guy, who carried a Buck knife on his belt, might be part of the Immigration Office of the federal government - the agency in charge of prosecuting the smuggling of illegal aliens into the United States.

Deliberately and in slow motion, DeJesus brought his hands together, fingers barely touching and wrists apart, then hands closer as if praying, and then fingertips to his lips as if deep in thought. In meetings, this gesture had always worked in getting a group's attention. Usually, they would cooperate and acquiesce to his demands, which he phrased in the form of suggestions.

"Let me suggest, that we continue the search for six more hours, until noon today, and then we reconvene with the notion that if nothing new has been discovered," pausing for dramatic emphasis, "we contemplate calling off the search." He looked around the circle, raising his black eyebrows, waiting for their response.

"Sounds acceptable," said the lead detective from the trooper barracks. His main concern was that he might injure or even lose one of his men.

"All right by me," the sheriff remarked as he turned to walk to the food truck to snag another doughnut.

"Sheriff, one thing," DeJesus said, addressing all nine of the men. "We tell the press we're continuing the search for six more hours, then we're meeting again, that's all." Everyone seemed to agree, and the administrators fanned out to the woods in the opposite direction of the press. They all had to go piss in the bushes. Too much caffeine. Even though the DEC had trucked up a sweet smelling port-a-potty, the men felt more like men when they urinated in the woods. Susie almost followed one of the detectives until she realized where he was going, and then she quickly veered away to talk to Tommy as he was being hoisted back into his hi-tech van.

"Why would someone want to escape from a minimum security place, I don't get it?" Susie asked.

"Are we on the record?" Tommy questioned in a jousting sort of way.

"We are, of course," Susie said, grimacing for fear she'd scare him off from whatever he had to say. She could always go off the record, and maybe get confirmation from another source.

"Off the record," Tommy mumbled knowingly, waiting. "No attribution."

"Oh, all right," Susie said, hoping to get something juicy.

"What is a federal border patrol official doing up here chasing a guy down into the mines? What the hell does he care? If you find that out, maybe you'll find out why the inmate ran." The aide was at the controls, turning the electrical engine on, withdrawing the mechanical platform bearing Tommy and his Hummer-chair, back into the van. Over the sound of the motor, and as the doors automatically slid shut on either side of him, Tommy looked up with his playful, cockeyed smile and said, "They're calling off the search."

Jeff Kelly

seventeen

Damian sat up in his hotel bed, disoriented. Where was he? He grabbed his watch - 6:30 a.m. Reveille was late, or his watch was wrong. Wait a minute, he was out. Free. He was free. He had a date today. He dropped back down to bed, rolled over in bliss and closed his eyes.

Late that afternoon, while sipping a Pepsi back out on the deck overlooking the lake, Pete told him that the prisoner who escaped ran down into the mines. After their conversation, Pete gave him a plaid work shirt to wear. It was the first wool shirt he had ever worn, red and black, making his black skin look light brown by comparison. Damian left for his rendezvous taking a leisurely route by the Miss Port Henry Diner, Sagan's, and across Main Street to the Chinese restaurant.

The town was in an altered state. Damian couldn't put his finger on it, maybe just fewer people on the streets. Those who were out appeared nervous, intent on getting where they were going, and less friendly. Damian assumed the shuttered mood had something to do with the escape, the first one since the prison opened its doors in 1989.

Damian walked by the miniature town park which was at the base of the hill up to Mineville. He turned up Broad past the Buttercup Florist walking the last few steps to the Golden Palace with his head down.

When he looked up, he was face to face with a six foot two, black, state trooper. A man standing next to the trooper introduced himself as a detective from the Bureau of Criminal Investigation. His grayish hair was a perfect brush-cut. The third man was Damian's C.O., Billy.

"You heard about the escape," Billy said. "The detective here wants to ask a few questions. They know you knew him. At least you worked on the same crew - my crew."

"I heard, but who escaped? "

"Klocks escaped, last night, about 8:00."

"Klocks, huh." Damian pulled back into himself, and instinctively, weighed the situation.

"Let's," the detective said, "take a moment and sit down inside. We just want to ask you a few questions."

Damian tried to compose himself, every few seconds looking over at the black trooper, the first African-American he had seen in the Adirondacks outside of prison. He was looking for a soul brother connection, a glimmer of recognition that in the larger scheme of things, they were on the same side. But he couldn't see the trooper's eyes behind his shades.

The trooper gestured with his hand for Damian to go inside the Golden Palace. Billy and the flat-top detective followed. They sat at the table next to the street window while the trooper remained standing with his arms crossed. He removed his shades and gave Damian a hard stare. Behind the counter, the Chinese guy who had wanted Damian to pay first, scowled, wondering what the hell was going on. Now there were two Negroes in his restaurant and one was the law.

A feeling of light-headedness settled on Damian. He raced back through events and conversations unsure if he was totally clean or not. Maybe Klocks had told him he was going to attempt something. But he couldn't remember anything specific. Damian Houser quickly decided that Wallace Klocks was way more savvy than he was. If Klocks had been planning an escape attempt, he wouldn't jeopardize it by telling another inmate. Damian calculated he had nothing to hide.

"You understand, Damian, we're just looking for information. Anything to help us figure out why a guy would try to escape one month before he was to be released." The detective was silent waiting for a response. But Damian wasn't biting. "Do you know anything?" the detective asked.

"No sir, he didn't say a word to me."

"He never spoke to you?"

"Oh, yes sir, he spoke to me. But nothing about escaping." This time Damian felt he had to fill the silence, give them something, so he continued.

"Only thing he said he believed in was 'the last word.'"

"What did he mean by 'the last word?'"

Damian hesitated and glanced up at the trooper. "He believed in retaliation and he believed in forcing others to dance to his music. He believed in payback. If someone or something wronged him, he would do whatever it took to get back at him. He called it 'the last word.'"

"Yeah, a lot of people in prison believe in 'the last word' - that's the problem," the detective remarked.

The Chinese cook, who was also the owner, edged around the counter, almost trembling. "Tea, you want tea? No charge for you."

The detective looked up from his blank notepad and replied. "Yeah, sure tea all around. Fortune cookies too. Right Damian? I understand Klocks didn't care for fortune cookies." Everyone forced a chuckle, even the trooper.

"Klocks went down into some godforsaken mine that I wouldn't go near for all the tea in China." When the Detective said China, he twitched his eyebrows and tilted his head in the direction of the Chinaman. "Did he ever mention the mines to you, Damian?"

"To me, never." Damian was startled by a tapping on the window next to his ear. It was Chantal with a baffled look on her face.

"Can I go?" Damian asked. "I can go, right? I hardly knew the guy."

"Sure, take off, kid. Wait." The detective reached for one of the fortune cookies and flipped it to Damian who was on his way out the door.

"Here," the flat-top said, "don't forget your fortune."

Damian one-handed the cookie and leaned against the purple king-cab. He crunched the shell, and without reading the fortune, tucked the tiny strip of paper into the breast pocket of his wool shirt.

"Hop in, "Chantal said. Nothing could dampen Chantal's mood, not even the roadblock she went through to get to Port Henry. "Did those guys hassle you? I've never seen so many cops and guys in suits. Not since that funeral for the Comstock guard. What did they want?"

"What did they want? Good question. I think they're a little suspicious of me, because of the timing."

"You mean, your being released the same day?"

"Hey, you got it."

"It's just a coincidence, right?" she asked sheepishly.

"Unless when he punched me at your place, he inserted a transmitter and I'm now his robot. I don't know, man. He's known as a guy not to be messed with."

"What do you want to do? Do you want me to show you around?"

"All right, sure let's just drive around. What about the ranch? What are my chances of working there?"

"Your chances are good. My mom said okay. You don't mind staying in the bunkhouse, do you? It's a little messy, but we can clean it up. I'll help you."

"All right, this is fat. What about pay?"

"You'll have to talk to my mother about that. We didn't get into it."

"Hey man. This is unbelievable. You've been great, setting me up like this. I won't let you down."

"I know you won't. What's your sign?"

"Virgo."

"I thought so. Either that or Scorpio. Mine's Aries."

Damian didn't know one thing about astrological signs. He knew about the Latin Kings and their eight pointed crowns. He knew the Bloods. But he didn't know Taurus and Libra and the rest. But he didn't tell Chantal that. Didn't know her well enough yet to disappoint her with his ignorance of the stars.

"I'll take you to Velez's Marina. We can get an ice cream and a hot dog there if you're hungry."

They drove down a steep hill, past an unpainted antique store. Damian slouched back and let the breeze on his face blow the grimaces away. He looked over at Chantal and realized he didn't know her last name. But that could wait.

He figured she probably didn't know his either. She was wearing an embroidered white cowboy shirt, blue jeans, a tight pair he now noticed, and moccasins.

"Where did ya get the moccasins?"

"A catalogue. L.L. Bean, I think. They used to sell them here at Sagan's, but Sagan's closed," she said as she drove into a dilapidated marina with more ornate junk around than Damian had ever seen. Chantal pointed out a glimmering Chris Craft wooden inboard on a trailer. Damian zeroed in on an antique, historic, bulbous-shaped fire truck, covered by a ripped blue tarp flapping in the breeze, parked forever next to a red, curved coke machine.

"Only fifty cents. Cheapest place I know to get a soda."

"Whoa,"Damian said, as she started to spin around the dirt turnaround. "I got fifty cents."

She completed her U-turn, and Damian got out. He inserted two quarters and out plunked one of those thick greenish bottles that only hold seven ounces. He flipped off the cap using the machine's built-in chrome bottle opener, the cap landing on the ground with all the other bottle caps imbedded in the packed dirt.

He gave the first sip to Chantal, and she duly noted that. Actually, prisoners in general were real conscious of good hygiene. They were acutely aware of the AIDS virus and suspicious of the literature that said you could only get it through blood and sex. Any bodily fluids is what Damian figured - 'Blood, Sweat and Tears.'

The coke was the first thing they shared. Damian could only hope they would share more. It occurred to him just then, after he took his first swig, that he didn't have any condoms.

For her part, Chantal watched Damian drink the coke and noticed that he was tidy in his appearance and careful in what he did or said. He was thin and tallish, maybe six feet, not pushy, kind of quiet. His learned look had first attracted her, that and the color of his skin. He could almost come off as an intellectual, especially when he wore his glasses.

She knew she was taking a chance, not with AIDS, but with hanging out with a black, ex-con. But life was passing her by. She was divorced, over thirty, back in Essex County with a Mom who dated younger men. Dating a black man, sleeping with a black man, would be about the only way she could demonstrate her individuality, and outdo her mother, not that that was her goal.

Damian strolled out on the dock and she followed, knowing to watch where she walked lest she put her foot through a plank. Velez's had seen better days much like the rest of Port Henry and Mineville. Chantal told how after Republic Steel closed the mines for good in 1971, Broad Street and Main Street were gloom and doom. Where there were three movie theaters, now there were none. Eight clothing stores, now there were two. Six car dealerships had dwindled to one, Wheelocks. And in the winters, when ice fishing was a religion, Wheelock's tow truck hoisted at least one unemployed, miner's pick-up from the bottom of the lake. If it weren't for Ti Mill and the logging industry, the town would have faded away like an Alaskan gold mining town. But it was coming back with a new convenience store and gas station called Stewart's, and the Essex County Ark. And, and of course, there was the prison. Yes, the town was thankful for all, otherwise it was doomed to be a museum of a mining town.

"We're still here, though," Chantal said smiling.

"I see that and I'm glad," Damian said looking her in the eye. They were at the end of the dock and the last rays of the setting sun were reflecting off the steel trusses of the Crown Point Bridge.

A few sailboats were moored beyond the dock, and at one slip a big man was polishing one long, gleaming, wooden inboard, a rare Hacker Craft. In back of him, inside an open post and beam barn, a row of copper and brass propellers, large and small, hung from the slanted wall, like trophies. They reminded Damian of a row of gaping shark jaws that he had seen in Montauk, Long Island. The rest of the barn was crammed with boats and pulleys and lathes and vices and enormous wrenches lying at all angles on the wooden counters. A man with white hair, with a huge gut and a huge head, wearing denim overalls and a T-shirt, limped along and looked up at Damian and Chantal to see if they wanted gas or something. Damian felt like an undersized visitor who had landed in a vague, timeless era anchored to some past decade.

"What do you want to do now?" Chantal asked, reaching down to dip her fingers in the water.

The 21 Mine

He looked at her, and thought about where he had been, and was afraid that if he pinched himself, he'd wake up. "I guess I want to get to know you."

Damian hesitated. He didn't want to ruin things by coming on too strong. He thought about kissing her. He touched her wet hand with his and she opened her mouth as if to say something, but then looked down at the planks of the dock, moving her foot in a semi-circle motion. At least they were holding hands, Damian thought, as they sashayed back to Mom's purple pick-up.

The man who had been polishing the boat caught sight of Damian, and then stood straight and tall, about six feet seven, as if to make sure he was seeing what he was seeing. He bellowed, "Well, young Damian, I'll be damned. They let you out. With all the action up there, I'm surprised they didn't put your ass back in. How the hell are you?"

Damian was caught off balance between his old prison world and his new free world. It was Spike Taylor, the drill instructor the inmates called Hurricane. The one who had throttled Klocks after he had karate-kicked the Oriental chef. "What did you think about Klocks?" Spike said as he walked over wearing a Cheshire-cat grin. "Klocks is something isn't he?"

Damian let Chantal's hand drop, feeling silly and self-conscious. He didn't know whether Hurricane was ready to turn on him or what. He'd never heard him talk like this. Before he had always roared a steady stream of 'Eyeballs' and 'Platoon Rise' and 'Platoon March.'

"Hi Spike," Chantal said demurely. She came up to his stomach, just above his black leather belt.

"Well Chantal, what's your mother going to say now?" Spike had his arm around Damian's shoulder and Damian was shrinking fast. "If she didn't like me, you think he's going to past muster," he said pointing to Damian and laughing heartily.

Damian wasn't sure if Spike was just having fun or being malicious. Spike took his arm off Damian's shoulder and turned and faced him, his bear-paw hand outstretched, "Congratulations, kid," Spike said. Damian guessed he was being sincere and shook his hand as best he could, quickly adjusting to the firmness of his handshake.

"Klocks is a wild man, isn't he? Why would he run into that pit?" Spike wasn't really asking Chantal and Damian that, rather he was just passing along news. "The fool only had one month left. Something's fishy. Witness protection program; that's what I say. He was meant to testify in federal court in Albany in ten days. What do you think, Damian?"

Damian was trying to relax, trying to accept that even guards smiled and had personal lives, and were all too human. But before Damian could respond, Spike continued. "What about you, Damian, staying around here, and then hooking up with my ex, here. You're something else."

Damian stiffened again and shot a glance at Chantal.

"He's just pulling your leg. We went out once in high school, but I wasn't fast enough for him, right, Spike?"

"Daz right," said Spike mimicking the prison talk of the brothers.

"Well, Spike," Damian said hesitantly, "Klocks didn't confide in me. But I know he wasn't afraid of any caves. He told me he once hid in a cave behind a waterfall for three days."

"Yeah, Billy said the vent he crawled out of was no bigger than his head. Shit, he'll love those mines."

The three of them stood there, and silence gave way to the awkwardness of a guard chatting with a former prisoner, and way back when, a former date. Always skillful in extricating herself, Chantal took Damian's hand, and said "I told Mommy," stressing Mommy to Spike, "that we'd be back by dinner. Bye Spike."

"Bye sweetie. And Damian," said Spike winking his eye, " if your hear from Klocks, tell him I meant him no harm."

As they walked away, Chantal muttered, "Yeah, now that he's escaped, they're all scared shitless he'll come after them."

Spike called out, "Awful strange you and Klocks being out on the prowl the same time. Damian."

Damian turned around, frazzled once again.

"Damian, anytime you want a ride in my boat, let me know. Seriously. No charge. This lake goes all the way to Canada. You let me know. This is one big lake."

eighteen

After walking a good distance from the main house, around behind an island of trees, Chantal pointed. "We call this the bunkhouse. It hasn't been used in a couple of months. There's not enough room in the house. And, you know, I don't think Heidi would let you stay there. Anyway, it's more private here."

Damian was mesmerized by the long paddock fence in the distance, remembering the hard work, thinking maybe he and Chantal and these mountains were all meant to be. In the center around the lone boulder, the mares were gathered, head to tail, swatting flies for each other, languishing in the cool breeze rising from underground.

He broke from his reverie and they meandered closer, gazing on the bunkhouse. From the outside, its singular feature looked to be a sod roof, which supported thick grass and even some wildflowers. Damian kicked away a cluster of pinecones and opened the painted red door.

"No problem, Chantal, this is great." What he meant was the whole situation was great. The cabin which Chantal called the bunkhouse needed to be swept of cobwebs, and the cot with wooden slats and a mildewed mattress was apt to be less comfortable than his bed at Moriah Shock, and certainly not as clean. But Moriah Shock had one schedule, theirs, and no divorced women.

Damian hadn't slept with many women. By ghetto standards, where most boys lose their virginity by age fourteen or fifteen, Damian was kind of prudish, not having done the deed until his last year of high school. Of course, once he got a taste of sex, it became his thing. He was always conniving with girls who had thought of him as a friend. There were a lot of bumbling propositions, coupled with awkward noes, but occasionally, maybe once every few months, one of the sophomore girls would whisper, 'Damian,' and giggle, dart a look around to make sure no one was watching, and then for fifteen seconds get serious and say, real fast, 'Come to my apartment, Friday, right after school. My mom won't be there.' The last girl became his girlfriend until he was sent Upstate.

Chantal held the door. "I'll help you clean it up. The main thing is the bathroom in the barn works."

"The main thing is I'm out and I'm with you."

Chantal smiled and didn't say anything, just kind of stroked the porch floor with her foot, like a filly.

"Chantal, you're a dream for me. And no matter what happens, you've given me hope." Damian hoped he wasn't bullshitting. Sometimes he lapsed into sweet-talking jive.

He reached across the space between them, which suddenly seemed like the Grand Canyon, and she stepped closer. He tugged her to him and hung his head to quietly kiss her. There's plenty of time, he repeated to himself, plenty of time.

Which there never was in the city, and usually there wasn't space either. There were only so many empty lots, and you couldn't go there at night, cause the girl couldn't relax and rightfully so. Too dangerous. And if it's daylight, it's like quick, quick, here comes somebody.

But here in the bunkhouse, talk about being alone. Nothing but birds and trees and horses around. Chantal had never kissed the lips of a black man. He kissed soft and gentle, side to side. She held her hands in front of her, on his ribs, trying to keep him at bay.

Damian released her, feeling light-headed. He gave out a little, "Whaoa!" and twirled in place, so unbelieving was he about his luck. He just didn't want to screw things up.

The 21 Mine

She snickered at his giddiness, stepping back out of the bunkhouse, pantomiming shooting him with her thumb and forefinger, feeling all right herself, and said, "dinner is in an hour."

The food turned out to be exquisite, kind of spicy Italian, which reminded him of city cooking, and the salads had fresh baby tomatoes from plants that Heidi had started in late winter in the greenhouse.

The main topic of conversation at the dinner table was the prison escape. Heidi zeroed in on Damian. "You knew this Klocks fellow, didn't you? Now, what's happened is just what I predicted would happen. An escaped prisoner who is dangerous. Now they're saying that he had a long record, that he's a con man and an informant. Damian, what's going on?"

Damian deferred more to an older woman, a mother-type figure, than to a man, and he fidgeted about with his fork before he answered. He actually stuttered a bit on the word I, and Chantal picked up on it. She had never heard him stutter. Some deep-rooted stress was coming to the surface, and this interested Chantal, and made Damian more intriguing, more complex to her. She noted the stuttering and kept quiet. "I, I didn't know Klocks that well, but he did, ah, talk to me. He was kind of a loner. I guess he was someone you'd watch out for. I know the Chinese didn't like him." He went on to tell them all about the fight in the mess hall. He thought the girls would laugh, but no one did. "I don't think he would harm anyone who wasn't out to get him. None of you are out to get him. So we're all safe, right?"

Damian thought that maybe he had gone too far, being a little flippant at the end, so he went back to trying to neaten-up the noodles he was twirling on his fork. Then, he took one of the largest bites of spaghetti that Chantal had ever seen a man take, and she and her sisters started to giggle. Damian, whose mouth was full, didn't know what they were laughing at - all laughing except the boss, Heidi, who hadn't yet sized up Damian to her satisfaction.

"Pass him the wine," she said coolly.

Damian nodded a thank you and gulped, and then, in a burst of self-consciousness, sipped the red wine. Shortly, he excused himself, and thanked them all for dinner, since he knew each of the sisters had helped cook. They were going off the hill into town for ice cream, some type of oreo flurry, but he said no thanks, and walked back to his bunkhouse to digest and close his eyes and dream. Half an hour later a crescent moon rose and there was an unexpected knock on his door. He was thrilled to see Chantal.

"Hey, Miss Chantal," he said playfully, "are you here to kiss me goodnight?"

She put her glass of wine down on the pine bureau and crossed her arms. "That's the first time I've heard you stutter," she said in a caring voice.

Damian shook his head in semi-disgust. She stood there waiting for some sort of explanation. "When I was a boy, you know seven-eight years old, I used to stutter. That's it, I got over it."

"Well, why did you stutter at the dinner table?"

"I didn't even know I did."

"Just a little, on the word I."

"When your mom was asking me about Klocks? I was nervous. Prisoners don't talk idly about other prisoners, that's how you get hurt."

"You mean, you know more about him than you told us."

"Yeah, well sure. But everything I told you was true."

"Will you tell me the rest?" She sipped her wine.

He looked at her dressed in blue jeans, sandals and a white, peasant blouse, and a few creases on her face. "In prison I tried not to think about women or old girlfriends. I tried to work so hard that I would fall asleep within minutes of lights out. Now I'm ready," he said lowering his head, bobbing slightly to an inner rhythm. He closed his eyes and hummed a tune. He opened his eyes and started singing a slow motion version of the House of the Rising Sun. She had never been sung to before.

He hopped down from the top bunk, and swung the door shut. Stepping a bit closer to him to get out of the way, she brushed him with her chest, and that's how the night began.

She reached up with her arms and lightly clasped them behind his neck, swaying to his heartfelt song. He held her waist, one hand feeling her cool, creamy skin under her blouse, the other clutching a handful of frilly fabric. This night when everyone else was in town, she had come to the bunkhouse for a reason, though she might not have admitted it to herself.

The 21 Mine

He was quivering slightly, out of pent-up energy and anticipation of a moment like this after six months in jail. Now was the time, to let his body and soul take over, and make the move. For only the second time since they had known each other, they kissed, strongly, holding a long time, pressing their lips hard against each other's. As she molded her body to his, he felt the mounds of her breasts against his hard stomach and chest. He was embarrassed at how quickly he was getting excited, but maybe she would understand.

"It's a, it's a," he stuttered.

"Been a long time?" she said finishing his words for him.

"So it might not be too good for you." he continued, as he slid both hands up underneath her blouse and forcefully grabbed her breasts.

"We'll see," she laughed, before she was knocked backward by his lunge at her breasts.

"Slow down tiger, I like this blouse," she said as button by button she undid it from the bottom up. He stood transfixed, waiting for the last button and her shirt to fall open.

He approached, and with a smooth languid touch slid the blouse down to the floor, adoring her white skin, knowing he would soon have her, alternating between the silky calmness of seduction, and the overwhelming push toward a natural orgasm that he had been deprived of for so long. She, more in control than he, caught the blouse with the toe of her right foot and deftly kicked it onto the lower bunk. Without a word, she contorted her arms behind her back, but when Damian figured out what she was doing, he said, "No, no, wait. Not yet."

God, he hadn't seen a bra and a partially clad woman in so long. And then he lost it, flinging her against the closed cabin door, sending the dead moths spiraling down from the window sill, fondling her, kissing her neck, and yanking the bra down around her waist, sucking and slurping on her tits. Matching the feverish pace, she undid his belt, and unzipped him, felt his hardness. They were both panting now. He ripped down her blue jeans, and fondled her pussy with his hand. She held his wrist and moaned. "Easy does it."

Moments later, breathing hard, he mumbled, "I'm sorry. I'm sorry, We'll do it again. It'll be better. More like love."

"You just about killed me. I only weigh a hundred and thirty."

He scooped up the flowered panties from the floor and ran them across his face, before flinging them on his top bunk. "They're mine." He squeezed her tits, rubbed her wonderfully flabby rear, and kissed her up and down her neck.

Chantal looked down at the pine floor at a swirling knot in the wood that reminded her of a Rorschach test her mother once forced her to take. Bravely, she looked up and regarded Damian's eyes as if he were her patient. She was feeling a bit awkward, almost like she, the older woman, was taking advantage of him. Looking back at their bout of lovemaking, if she could call it that, Chantal felt an unwanted pressure on them, marking the beginning of the end of their idyllic days.

* * * *

Two days passed before they were alone and together again after this first sexual outburst in the bunkhouse. In the meantime, Damian was actually enjoying the casual routine around the farm and discovered that shoveling horse manure out of stalls wasn't that bad, as long as you thought about something else while you were doing it and didn't take it personally.

It was in the barn next to the stall of a horse named Banner, that he found the nail gun resting on a cross beam. Now that he was free, he could fire that nail gun. And he did, pleased to find it was still loaded with twelve-penny nails. He took the gun with him back to the bunkhouse.

On the third day, Damian walked a yearling called Brush Strokes out to the paddock that his crew had built. The paddock had become his favorite place on the ranch to work and hang out. He liked the thought that he had made something permanent, a monument of sorts. Twenty five years was permanent to a young convict. He'd walk around the paddock inspecting the fence, touching the posts that he had dug the holes for, thinking that maybe he'd like to go to Havana, Florida, where the pressure-treated posts were made. It sounded like an exotic place.

Chantal wandered out with a newspaper and some sugar cookies in a ball jar, reminding him of the first time he had seen her out there, and the ruckus she caused.

"Here, you'll like these, they're sweet," Chantal said in a sing-song way.
"Like you?"

"Like me," she said, hanging her head and smiling, liking the way he flirted.

She sat and undid the top of the glass bell jar. "Was that your mother who called last night?"

"Yep, she was begging me to come home. A buddy of mine died. A kid from the streets."

She stretched on the grass in the middle of the paddock not too far from the boulders and trees and the underground breeze. "Well, what happened?" she asked while she tugged on the cuff of his blue jeans, motioning for him to sit as she untied her sneakers.

Damian told Chantal about his history with Reginald and what had happened. They had been friends since grade school. Well, Reginald at age twenty-two, was, until a week ago, the toughest, slickest drug dealer selling crack cocaine who had yet to be sent Upstate. Reginald had absolutely no respect for, nor fear of authority, which was his downfall.

The incident that sent him to an early grave happened in the downstairs hallway of a dilapidated tenement building. Reginald was doing a deal, selling drugs, when an undercover Irish detective named Sheridan walked in and flashed his badge. In an instant Reginald pulled out his nine inch stiletto, and crouched in knife-fighting position. Sheridan was ready to reach around back for his gun holstered in the small of his back. The buyer was cowering in the back of the hallway looking for a way out.

Sheridan was a tough Irish detective. He said to Reginald, 'You make one move and I'll take that knife and shove it up your ass.'

Reginald was no fool. He knew he was caught selling drugs. He didn't know Sheridan, and Sheridan didn't have a gun in his hand.

'With what?' Reginald said as he swiped across the front of Sheridan with his knife and then lunged. Sheridan fell backward, drawing his revolver, taking a deep cut across his left forearm. He fired five times, killing Reginald.

"Reginald's wake is Wednesday, in two days. The user was a harmless old crack head. They let him go and he told Ma the whole story."

Chantal listened as she picked out single blades of green grass from the field.

"Ma's using the wake to entice me back home. The whole neighborhood will be there, all the old thugs, free on bail. What Ma doesn't understand is that's the problem. Things are going good for me here in the hills of the Adirondacks," he said with some aplomb. Damian's eyes drifted proudly toward Chantal and then the horizon. He ran his hand through her straight, brown hair and then down her back.

At least for now, he had Chantal. Why should he leave to go back? Up here, nobody bothered him, so far. All the mountain folk seemed to leave him alone. Didn't seem that interested in him. Which is the way he liked it. Really, in the short run, Moriah Shock had made a difference. He had gained some discipline and self-respect.

The only wild card was Klocks. The guy scared him and he didn't want to get entangled in the escape. Damian puzzled over the whereabouts of Klocks' family. Usually, when there's an escape, the mother shows up to await the outcome. Kind of like showing up at the trial to await the verdict of the jury. In an escape attempt the verdict was almost always captured dead or captured alive, but hardly ever not found, escaped, disappeared, or presumed dead.

The Plattsburgh Press Republican which had been covering the story on a daily basis quoted a trooper as saying, "He's probably dead. There's ten different mine shafts he could have fallen down."

nineteen

Slabs of shale and nodules of iron ore had fallen from the ceiling creating a boulder choke which blocked access to the bat's passageway. Klocks kneeled and shoved rocks aside, feeling perhaps too confident that the searchers wouldn't hear. And if they did, the sound was just more collapsing rock in a mining complex crisscrossed by cracks from years of blasting.

He cleared away much of the breakdown, before he stopped and ate one bite of his banana. Anything he could do to strengthen his inner resolve, to prove that he was special and different, he did. He took some long, slow breaths, in through the nose, out through the mouth, and prayed his intuitive powers would see him through the coming ordeal. What were his chances of finding a way out? While he was meditating on the long odds, some sort of crustacean scurried over his thigh.

Oblivious, Klocks stared upward at the barely visible cavern ceiling, a coppery hue of alternating bands of dark and light colors, reminding him of strips of bacon. His stomach growled. Stop stalling and start crawling, he thought. "I'm the Owl; I can make it."

Klocks had followed the bat and found a finger raise, a small opening above a stope, or excavation, through which miners lugged iron ore. In he went, headfirst, crawling on his elbows, his flashlight in one hand, his bag in the other.

He kicked rocks back around the hole to cover up the opening as much as possible. He prayed he wasn't wasting his energy down another dead end.

He flicked off the waterproof flashlight and slithered onwards until he was able to rise to his knees, and finally crouch. Like a troglodyte, all instinct and senses, he lurched his way downward along the wet scree and squishy guano. I've been in worse places, he thought, like the vent I squeezed out. The finger raise narrowed again until he was forced to crawl. His feral nature surfaced. He sensed a drop-off, feeling ahead until his hands gripped the edge. He pulled his body the last few feet and turned on the flashlight.

He was awed by what he saw. A massive chamber larger than any room he had ever seen. His whole cell block at Moriah Shock could have fit inside. Tunnels and shafts angled in and out from all directions.

The maze of openings confused him and his hand-drawn map would prove to be of little help, but Klocks' spirits were buoyed by the prospect of walking upright. His immediate problem was how to descend the thirty feet to the floor of the chamber. He thrust his upper body out of the hole, and like a trapeze artist ready to swing, hung there upside down holding the flashlight in his mouth.

In difficult rock climbing situations like this he had learned to picture a series of moves and then act quickly, not to over-analyze. Otherwise a kind of paralysis set in making the first move a terrifying, endless wait.

While sticking out of the hole, he moved around until he was facing upward toward the dome ceiling. Tensing his abdominal muscles, he curled up at the waist, doing a sit-up in the air, feeling and rubbing above the opening for a handhold. He found the beginning of a chimney, a vertical crack in the rock wall, which widened upward. Wiping away the slime, he wedged both hands in at the bottom of the crack, sliding his lower body out of the finger raise, and dangling his legs in space across the opening. From there he turned and tilted his head downward so that the flashlight illuminated the cavern floor. Swinging out, pivoting off the wall with one foot, yanking out his hands, he jumped away from the wall and down to what looked to be the cleanest landing. When he hit, he rolled and banged his head on the footwall.

He shook his head to stay conscious because he knew to be knocked out could be the end. If it weren't such an ignominious ending, he might have accepted it. But Klocks, the Owl, did things in style, and called his own shots. If he was going to die, he wanted the front page, not an underground chamber where no reporters would ever find him and endangered Indiana bats would cover him with guano until he turned to fertilizer.

Woozy, Klocks wobbled to his feet. He picked up his rubber flashlight, and shone it around, reeling at the size of this room and its towering pillars, incredibly large to be enclosed underground. He stumbled about in reverence, as if inside a bombed cathedral from a forgotten war.

Next to a shaft with rotten timbers sticking up out of the opening, Klocks found a wheelbarrow, remarkably intact, with elongated handles and three sides of a wooden box up front near the wheel. Years ago, wheelbarrows were used by muckers to dump the ore directly into the skip coming up out of the shaft. Beyond the wheelbarrow, an overturned skip, a giant bucket the size of a dead combat tank, sat, its seized-up wheels exposed to the still air.

The gloomy scene imprinted itself on his telepathic sense. People died here, Klocks thought. He cleared and emptied his mind while his psychic senses filled the vacuum. Klocks started walking in circles listening to the words, the silent voices. He shone his light on the shaft, and kicked a chunk of iron ore down it. He counted, one-one thousand, two-one thousand, until he heard a muffled splash. A few more years and even this mammoth cavern would start to fill with water.

Klocks looked up and saw a twisted rail coming out of a drift, or side tunnel. On the floor below, jumbles of coiled cable were strewn about near a jackhammer and a twenty pound sledge. As he absorbed the images, his eyes went blank and the trance washed over him.

* * * *

Three men are sending a skip of iron ore on rails up the shaft. They stop, chew tobacco, and spit. Above the whir of the slusher hoist motor they hear the growing roar and concussion of a runaway skip charging down the chute, in free fall. They scatter. The loaded ore skip, weighing twenty-nine tons, crashes through a protective bulkhead, going 350 miles per hour, and explodes into the room, sending debris flying, killing two. One immigrant is beheaded and the other dies calling out in Polish the names of his daughters, while five bells toll three times and the survivors wait for the hoistman to signal all clear for an exit cage.

* * * *

This dark vision made Klocks want to clear his head and search for his own exit. Klocks quickly realized he would need to rely more on his mental powers, vision and toughness, than in his youthful past when his substantial physical prowess conquered all.

Light was key to his escape yet Klocks turned off his flashlight. He felt for the candle and matches. Candlelight was different, less focused and far reaching, but more telling in one regard - the flame revealed the slightest of breezes, and Klocks knew that a breeze came from the mix of air in the mine with air from outside. Slowly, he walked the perimeter of the large chamber, sloshing through water, around piles of muck and crushed rock, eager for a waft of air or the fluttering shadow of a bat. Klocks stopped every few seconds to observe the flame so he wouldn't mistake his own movement for that of a genuine breeze.

He tripped on some tangled cables. Miners must have been desperate to work down here, he thought. He'd rather do time. He was part way around the oblong room when he sensed sound waves and stopped. Was it a bat navigating above him? He held the candle aloft, imagining himself the Statue of Liberty. He was proud to be a United States citizen, proud of his Italian/Irish heritage, and proud that he knew every word to the Star Spangled Banner, not like Damian who never opened his mouth during the Star Spangled Banner. Who did he think he was? Klocks began to sing, in a hoarse whisper, "Oh! say, can you see, by the dawn's early light, What so proudly we hailed at the twilight's last gleaming? Whose broad stripes and bright stars through the perilous fight . . ." and then he hushed. The flame was flickering. He wasn't sure if it was from his singing or a breeze. He kept the candle high above and as still as the great lady herself. The flame burned straight and Klocks fought off a sinking depression. He walked three paces, and again held the candle aloft. He raised his head and the flame was bending and dancing to a draft of cold air falling from somewhere above. "Yesss," he hissed.

Now to prepare to climb in search of a passage with an opening to the outside. The miners called it an adit. He snuffed out the candle, kissing it before he tucked it away in his bag, and pulled out the flashlight, scanning the wall with its beam for the source of the tantalizing draft of air.

Halfway up, about sixty feet, he detected the remnants of a miner's ladder bolted to the gneiss and granite rock. Adirondack miners called it black rock. The rock contained some quartz and mica, but no iron ore. It was, however, good climbing rock.

Klocks was proud but guarded about his Houdini-like traits. When handcuffs and leg irons were brought to bear, he could swell the size of his wrists and ankles, and slip out of the shackles later. He had control of his toes the way the average man had control of his fingers. He could undo handcuffs and turn combination locks with his toes. Most convicts would have bragged about these traits, but Klocks never did. He believed in secrets, and secrets were between he and himself and nobody else. Once you told somebody else, it was no longer a secret. He was a snitch himself, and recognized that no man could be trusted when a detective was dangling a reduced sentence in front of him.

Klocks felt another wave of exhaustion and hunger. Sensing that he was on to something, he sat down right where he was standing and curled up in a ball on the cold rock and slept. For how long, he had no idea. When Klocks awoke, the darkness was so balack he wasn't sure he was awake. He fumbled in his pack and found his flashlight.

Wallace Klocks opened his mouth and gripped the flashlight with his teeth. He rubbed his hands, jiggling them around, the same ritual he used before opening a safe. He twisted his neck, turning the light on with his tongue and scanned high up on the rock wall. He saw indentations, some blacker shadows, but he couldn't be sure what was what. He'd just have to climb. Too bad he didn't have a rope and some carabiners and pitons - hardware for rock climbing. He never had the right equipment at the right time; he always improvised.

The rock wall was rough with small cracks and imperceptible outcroppings. In no time, he was up thirty feet, breathing hard. The knuckles on his right hand were chaffed and bleeding, but he expected that. He kept the light on, though the batteries were precious. Finding a way out, now, on this attempt, was crucial.

Spread out like a spider, Klocks was taking a break on the hanging wall, actually leaning back from the black rock, knowing that if he fell he'd probably die. He was alone and on his own and that was the way he liked it.

Wallace Klocks had been on his own since a truck driver named Horace moved in with his mom when he was sixteen. From the get-go Klocks didn't like Horace. Didn't like hearing Mom's creaking bed, so he left the tenement with its peeling paint and propane odor and became his own man of the streets; a master criminal he called himself.

As an adult, Klocks was respected in the Upstate world of crime for his knowledge of antiques. During an early winter he might spend the whole day with his van parked quite visibly in the driveway of a house in Upstate New York - in Cambridge or Greenwich, or even nearby Westport; summer homes owned by people from the city, from Manhattan. Carefully, he would evaluate all the furniture and paintings, before stealing the best. No one bothered him, he was so brazen about it. It was the damn people he fenced to who gave him trouble. Sometimes they didn't respect all the work and drudgery he went through, and that's when he became resentful; when they wouldn't give him the price he wanted. He had gone overboard a few times; he admitted it. That's why he didn't like carrying a gun; he was apt to use it.

Puffing out his cheeks, he exhaled long and slowly, expelling the intrusion of thoughts from the past, collecting himself for returning to the present. He concentrated on one sweaty, cold cheek, and then the other, trying to sense the slightest movement of air - trying to find the down draft that the candle had signaled to him was here somewhere high on this chamber wall.

A big brown bat appeared and he watched carefully. He had lost track of time, but he knew bats didn't. Either the bat was headed outside for a night of hunting mosquitoes, or inside to sleep for the day. The bat darted in and out of the flashlight's beam and then seemed to disappear somewhere up to his left. That's where he headed. He was committed. He doubted he'd be able to climb back down. He wished he too had a membrane attached to his fingers. "Why can't the Owl use his wings?" he mused. He focused on each handhold, on each foothold, as he traversed higher diagonally across the rock.

His weaker right leg, where years ago he had torn his hamstring running across a frozen swamp away from the cops, was shaking from fatigue. He always escaped to the worse places, where sedentary cops never liked to follow. He lost them in swamps, in dense woods, down rivers and now in mining caves, losing them, he hoped, forever.

His left foot tight on an inch-wide granite ledge, Klocks made a fist with his left hand and jammed it into a crevice, turning it like a screw, scraping the skin off his knuckles while locking his hand in place. Then he took the weight off his vibrating right leg, allowing the leg to hang freely and stretch.

Ordinarily, when climbing, he liked to have three points of contact. He composed himself by breathing deeply. He was getting close to where the bat had disappeared. Weakened and dizzy from the exertion and little to eat, he didn't look down, too high up. The shadowy depths might unnerve him further.

For the first time, he clearly saw two pieces of wood parallel to each other - the decayed ladder. More carefully than ever he picked his way in that direction. He was forced to make one foolish move, where he had no footholds, and was hanging by his hands. The toe of his left shoe hit an object, and he tested it, putting more and more weight on it, finally believing in it. He looked down at his foot to see what he was standing on. It was a rusted bolt of iron protruding from the wall. Something man-made, probably a pin for the ladder. He looked above and saw the wood sides without the rungs. A pattern emerged; every four feet, there was a nub of iron.

He had found the route the miners took when bolting in their ladders to set dynamite charges atop the rich magnetite pillars. Their aim was to explode and sever the pillars from the ceiling, so the iron ore could be mined. The remaining wood was probably forty years old and definitely no good; a moist fiber that came apart in his hands. But the iron bolts were still solid and secure enough for support. He patted the cold rock with his hands until he found regular indentations - handholds that must have been carved with tools when the miners went through their high wire, time-consuming task of constructing a catwalk high on this monumental, man-made face of black rock.

He angled upward a few feet at a time, gradually finding an awkward rhythm, gaining elevation. The higher he climbed, the more desperate and determined he became. The pebbles he sent flying were like a delicate waterfall, distant ting-a-lings reminding him of how incredibly high-up he was. Soon, even the rungs of the ladder were in place, but they too fell apart in his hand and were more of a hindrance than a help. He was dripping in sweat yet chilled. He lost his focus and stopped, gingerly supporting himself with shaking legs pressed against wet, encrusted iron nubs.

He closed his eyes and when they blinked open, a bat with the face of a mongrel dog took shape and emerged directly above his head, flapping onto his hair. He let out an "Auugggh," but didn't dare move to swipe it away. Both hands were pressed outward on subtle outcroppings to keep himself from falling. The furry bat entangled its winged fingers in Klocks' hair, screeching like a baby and Klocks went trance-robotic, closed his eyes and froze.

Like magic, the bat disappeared and Klocks opened his eyes and pulled his head back a few inches from the rock wall. He chuckled softly and then laughed loudly. He felt a distinct cool breeze across his tangled hair. He adjusted the position of the flashlight through the grime in his mouth, stretched his legs to stand on his tiptoes, raised his body another four inches, performing an iron cross, and with his forehead bashed the wall again and again. More and more dirt and stones streamed down, along with an increasing volume of water. He was enlarging the crumbling hole the bat had flown out of. He was sure he had found his way out.

Soon the hole was bigger than his head. He craned his neck and shone in the flashlight. He was at the beginning of a small adit. A torrent of surface water poured out and over him, enlarging the hole. Klocks' glee turned to terror as he saw he could be swept to his death by the rush of water. Mustering his last burst of strength, he flung himself into the hole, breaking through rubble with his shoulders, landing with his face underwater, chipping a tooth and knocking the flashlight from his mouth. He kicked and squirmed farther in, fearing the edge underneath him might collapse. Sputtering to his knees and elbows, crawling in a small streamway, struggling forward, he lifted up his eyes and started cackling, not bothering to retrieve the flashlight. It was shining and twirling underwater, rolling toward the widening opening at his feet and the plunge to the base of the mammoth chamber.

Klocks was scrambling in the opposite direction toward the most glorious sight gleaming through the darkness. It was a light hole. At the far end of this streamway, hard to tell how far, maybe five hundred feet, maybe one thousand feet, he glimpsed a pinprick of daylight. "The Owl," he wailed. "The Owl has arrived."

With relief and weariness, Klocks' neck muscles loosened and his face fell back into the streamway. The rain water flowed into his open mouth, down his throat. He rolled over on his back exhausted and bloody, still shaking. With the strength that comes from seeing the end in sight, he got up as best he could, in a kind of Neanderthal stance, scraping his back and banging his head on the passageway, stumbling, splashing, crawling toward the daylight, with the preternatural instinct of a baby at birth, intent on making it through the light hole.

Jeff Kelly

twenty

"**L**ook at the headlines," Chantal said as she opened the newspaper. "Heidi's furious. This is what she was afraid of. She's already phoned the Warden." The headline said, 'Search For Escaped Prisoner Called Off.' The byline was Susie's and a highlighted pull quote blared, 'No one could survive down there,' attributed to a sheriff's deputy.

Damian scanned the article and shook his head in mild disbelief. "Nobody could survive down there except Klocks," he joked half-heartedly. "They have no idea what a desperate man's capable of. Klocks in those mines is like throwing Br'er Rabbit into the brier patch."

Damian put down the paper and tilted his head in the direction of the puffy blackish clouds in the evening sky. "Those look like the clouds I used to draw in elementary school." He put his arm around Chantal and she cuddled closer. Damian liked her because he could tell her things he'd never tell a man, things he could never say in prison. But she listened like they were pearls of poetry from Langston Hughes. He kissed her ever so softly on her neck. A strong, warm breeze, kept the flies away. Damian rolled on his back and flung his arms out to the side. "I'm in heaven."

Chantal waited, not wanting to break the spell. Then suddenly Damian sat upright, and she took that as an opportunity to talk business. "Heidi wants you to build another fence inside the paddock - much smaller; around the tree and that hole in the ground. She's afraid one of the yearlings will break an ankle."

147

Damian was silent, as they both contemplated the boulder and the saplings. He spoke slowly in a distant, monotone voice. "Yeah, that would be a good idea."

Something was stirring inside him and his eyes were widening. Chantal picked up on his abrupt mood change. "Is everything okay, honey?"

He put his finger to his lip as he whispered shhhh. Finally, as Chantal looked around at the pastoral setting, she concentrated on listening. She heard the swish of a horse tail, the brushing of pine needles in the wind, and in the background an engine, probably Heidi's pick-up.

"There," Damian said, both fingers raised to the darkening sky as he looked at the ground. Something had welled up in Damian before he heard anything. Some force, some earthly message had reached Damian's subconscious, and had sat him upright. Now he needed corroboration from his senses and if possible from Chantal too. "It's kind of a scraping sound, like you get digging holes for those posts."

Chantal wanted to hear something, but she couldn't ferret out the sound Damian was describing. She fastened her eyes onto Damian and didn't like the troubled look on his face, the furrows on his forehead.

Then they both heard a muffled groan and Damian spun around, spooked, ready to face an invading spirit. Chantal heard the groan too and stood up next to Damian, grabbing his forearm. The front page of the newspaper was blowing across the field, and hesitantly, Damian followed, walking toward the aspen trees and the boulder where the cool air blew from the hole.

Chantal walked behind in her bare feet and then froze. "Damian, I felt something." She stopped motionless, trying to come up with an apt description. "Something moved. I felt a vibration under my feet."

"What the fuck is happening?" Damian said, losing his cool, having quickly left heaven.

And then a loud, audible, animal-like groan, caught them like a lightning strike in a storm. They both felt awfully exposed out in the center of the field with nothing to hide under or behind. Damian grabbed Chantal's wrist and they jogged toward the only shelter in the paddock, where the horses gather for the shade and the cool, underground breeze.

The 21 Mine

"Are there any animals around here?" he called back to her. "Any wolves, any mountain lions?"

"I don't know," she said breathlessly, "There're coydogs."

"What are they?"

The next part of this memorable day was etched in their eyes in slow motion. As they ran closer to the cluster of trees surrounding the hole, something moved there down in the dirt, almost as though the ground itself were cracking and a prehistoric plant was powering its way to daylight.

Chantal and Damian abruptly halted with arms spread, almost toppling over, their hands brushed and they grabbed each other's wrist, eyes wide open. They were caught in the center of the field, and all they could do was drop and freeze.

From the hole, a miner's tiny finger hole from a bygone era, emerged some sort of dirt-encrusted paw, or was it a grimy hand? Then a contorted shoulder, and then a head blacker than Damian's, caked and matted with iron ore tailings, with two closed slits for eyes. Like a giant mole, the creature fell back inside.

Flattened into the field, still holding each other, Chantal had no notion of what was going on, but Damian's mind was flashing with an unwanted reality. The past was coming to get him. From the hole, a deep hyena-like laugh began. Damian had heard a sound like this before. The creature burst forth from the hole, on all fours, filthy, crawling in circles, looking everywhere, seemingly satisfied, cackling, and now rolling around on the ground, laughing.

The maniacal mutterings transformed into a voice, and Damian's evil premonition from the lake had come to pass. His frolic in heaven on earth had been stamped out. He turned to Chantal and looked at her with the oddest, saddest look a man had ever given her. The flicker of happiness that she had witnessed was gone, and their lives would never be the same.

The creature, who was metamorphosing into a man, was stumbling up, cagey and joyous. He fell back to his knees, his eyes adjusting to the light, and grabbed clumps of grass, mumbling, "The Owl, the Owl has done it." And finally with the utmost glee, he uttered, "I'm still the man."

Damian knew now. He threw off Chantal's hand, in anger at what fate had dealt him, stood straight, and marched over to Klocks.

At the edge of the dirt track surrounding the paddock, the wrinkled, inside pages of the newspaper were stuck in the tangled underbrush, except for the folded front page with the headlines about the search being called off, which had fluttered away, soaring on some higher draft atop the pinnacle of the pines, free as the printed word can be. Klocks was unaware of the headline and the irony of that page flying high.

"Together again," Klocks said gleaming. Damian was dumfounded and whirled with a fierce look of dejection to Chantal who was holding back, motionless.

"I almost died," Klocks moaned, rubbing his eyes.

Then Klocks noticed the woman farther away in the field. He eyed Damian who shrugged his shoulders, as if to say, she's not involved. She's not a good guy, she's not a bad guy, she's not one of us.

"That's Chantal. Remember when we worked on the fence. Remember the babe who brought the food. That's her."

"Ain't you something," Klocks said absent-mindedly, distracted by his own body and its needs. "I see. I was right," squinting, shading his eyes, looking around at the paddock fence and the two yearlings he had scared away. "It was connected." He looked up at Damian. "There's a whole world under there. Maybe I'll go back down." He laughed. "I need something to eat."

Damian looked at Chantal, pleading for some understanding of his plight. Chantal now realized that this was the escaped prisoner they had been reading about. She dusted herself off, thinking that it hadn't rained in weeks. Without too much thought or heavy weighing of alternatives, she stepped closer and said she'd be right back with some water and food.

First, she came back with a towel and a bucket of water from the spigot for the horses. "You'll want to clean up," she said. "You're blacker than Damian."

Klocks liked her comment. He turned his hands over and stared at his forearms all covered in the black dust of iron ore. The same particles which coated the lungs of the miners and sent them to an early grave, a few even glad to go, welcoming the eternal rest from their grim life.

"How many days has it been?" Klocks asked of Damian.

Damian wasn't sure what time frame he was referring to.

Klocks was drinking the water from his dirty, cupped hands, before he splashed some on his face. "Since I escaped. How much time has gone by? You lose track down there."

"More than three days," Damian said calmly.

And then with the resignation of an accomplice and the perverse pride the public takes in a skillful prison escape, Damian gave Klocks the good news. "The paper says they've called the search off. They think you're dead. Dropped down one of those shafts."

"I should be dead." The white towel was now spotted black from Klocks wiping the soot away. "Thank God for prison libraries, my memory and maps. And yeah, for bats, for fucking bats, man. They led me out. They led the way."

"The endangered Indiana bat," Damian remarked, showing a prideful disdain about the knowledge he gleaned from the newspaper coverage.

Klocks was on his knees rubbing the last of the soot from his face, dipping the towel in the bucket, loosening up a bit, swatting the black flies in the stillness of the coming night. He covered his face in the towel, and let out a muffled sob, which Damian first mistook for a smothered sneeze.

Damian had never seen that from Klocks, certainly not in prison.

"I'm spent," Klocks mumbled. "But that's good news, good news. Now maybe they'll leave me alone."

On his knees he reached out to touch the hand of Damian. Damian pulled back a second, and then Klocks said "Help me up. Maybe tonight's a blue moon, because I'll tell ya, never again. It was will, will power and luck that got me here. I couldn't do that again, even in my prime. It was once in a blue moon." Klocks looked up at the coming night sky and the barely visible north star, and collapsed, leaning weakly against the gray, granite boulder. "It was in the stars."

Admittedly moved, but always wary of a con-man, especially a resourceful one like Klocks, Damian was alarmed. Klocks knew how to control situations and people. Damian worried about what was next, seeing how quickly he was losing control while Klocks gained.

"Food, I need some food," Klocks said patting his scraped and hardened stomach. And then under his breath to Damian, "Is she all right? She won't rat?"

Jeff Kelly

twenty one

Chantal at five foot six was just about as tall as Klocks, and she didn't know what to make of him, nor he of her. He had always felt there wasn't a woman he couldn't eventually charm or con. He had actually moved in with a girlfriend of one of his cronies, a petty thief in Balston Spa. The guy had disappeared, thanks to Klocks, who was afraid the guy might give him up for a reduced sentence. So he knocked him off, and after he convinced the guy's girlfriend that her man had run out on her, knocked her up. Klocks had strangled the guy right after he had pawned some antique silver they stole. Klocks was angry at how little cash, something like two hundred dollars, he had gotten for the silver. He was convinced his partner was holding back some money and might rat. So he strangled him, doubling his own share.

Chantal loved Damian's foreignness, his blackness, and his idealism. Klocks was not as foreign to her as he might have guessed. He reminded her of her first husband - a real loser, who to this day came around asking to borrow money. Chantal knew she had a weakness that men liked, especially men like Klocks. She had a gullible quality, a certain innocence she retained that made her appear younger than she actually was. She was thirty-four, eight years younger than Klocks and twelve years older than Damian. She wanted to trust people. It was too much work for her to always be skeptical, always trying to figure what angle someone might be playing. She liked her trustworthy side. Both men and women confided in her, and generally she kept their secrets.

Jeff Kelly

She sensed immediately to watch out for Klocks, that he had been around the block too many times, and probably couldn't stop himself, probably was a pathological liar without realizing it. Couldn't help himself. He would say whatever was required to meet his objective. Klocks was always slightly puzzled when he heard from people on the street that so and so was after him for money he owed or to avenge a friend whom he had double-crossed and sent Upstate on his testimony. Didn't they understand that he was looking out for himself first. Wasn't that natural? How else did you survive. If a state police senior investigator offered him no time, versus three years in jail, to wear a wire, then he'd wear a wire. Who wouldn't?

Well the answer was, most wouldn't. Most cons would do time rather than fink on a partner or rat on their brother. The retribution in prison was heavy duty, usually a shiv in your ribs, and then there was the constant tension of looking over your shoulder. But Klocks was a loner anyway, wasn't afraid of anyone, and if given a chance, could talk his way out of most situations. He was well connected to the world of burglars and fencers, and cops made bonuses off having him as an informant.

Chantal knew that Klocks was a thug and Damian wasn't. As far as Chantal was concerned, Damian was doing time for smoking joints, something her mother, Heidi, did to this day with her artsy-fartsy friends. It came home to her that life wasn't always fair. Just like John F. Kennedy said. It occurred to her that the Kennedy family was still paying the price. But here she was aiding and abetting a criminal, an escaped con. The only way she could justify it was that he was presumed dead, so as far as she knew, he was dead.

Especially since Klocks, overjoyed with his disappearance, his official demise, had decided to change his name to Deed Rivers. Deed for having done the deed, making a miraculous escape, and for having been an 'a' away from d-e-a-d, dead. Rivers for the river of life in his favorite song by Billy Joel.

Between bites Klocks said, "I need time to think and a place to stay? Can you two do that for me?"

"Sure Klocks, sure," Damian said.

"Deed, it's Deed."

The 21 Mine

"Okay, Deed. But you know, I'm out on probation. I don't want any trouble. I'm not a career guy," he paused afraid to make him mad, "like you."

Klocks looked at him with tired eyes, "And a place to say. I need to sleep." Klocks' legs were starting to cramp up from the long climb up the cavern wall. "Sister, help me up." He looked to Chantal for help, but Damian stepped forward and lifted him by his armpits.

Both Chantal and Damian saw that they were into it now. This threesome would have a life of its own. Back to the bunkhouse they trudged.

"I suppose we can keep this from Mom. She never comes out here," Chantal said.

Damian quickly turned his head and stared at her, as if to say, 'Yes she does come out here. She might come out here any day now.'

Damian was silent, thinking no more lovemaking here, thinking I'll kill him if he touches her, afraid of him at the same time, knowing he was a real crook, and Damian was still growing up hoping for a third and fourth chance to redeem himself. This was not the way for his salvation. He didn't want to become what he was becoming.

Klocks was comatose with exhaustion. He uncurled his cramped fingers and let go a sparkling chunk of iron ore that he had snagged in his last dash up the streamway. They put him in Damian's lower bunk, and threw a horse blanket over him. "Perfect, this is perfect," he moaned as he passed immediately into a deep sleep. The weighty, fist-size chunk of ore remained on the pine bureau until Klocks left for good.

Damian and Chantal stepped outside, and shoved the pine board door shut. They looked at each other with troubled expressions. "We could turn him in?" Chantal offered.

"Deed. What a stupid-assed name. Have you ever heard of anyone called Deed?" Damian said, avoiding the more important issues.

Damian needed time to think clearly. "Let's drive into town and get some Chinese."

Chantal drove. They were both stupefied.

"What are you going to do?" Chantal asked in a hoarse whisper.

"You mean what are we going to do?" Damian snapped back.

Chantal reached over and put her hand on his knee "Let's not argue," she said soothingly.

Damian slammed his fist against the dashboard. "It's not fair. It's not fair. Everything was going great."

They were quiet as they rumbled over some frost eves on Plank Road. Gloom was setting in.

"The first thing I saw was this grimy paw. I thought it was a goddamn troll. And then I saw it was a hand." He paused as it registered. "The telescope," he said, shaking his head.

"What telescope?" Chantal repeated. "The telescope," he said through gritted teeth.

"Remember I told you about what I saw out on the Lake before we met. God damn it! The fucking thing has come to pass. We're going to the Champ Hotel right now."

Chantal didn't say a word because she did remember. And she was a little freaked.

She parked the purple king-cab in the Grand Union lot and they walked into the hotel lobby. Damian hit the desk bell. "Pete," he called. "It's Damian. The guy from the prison." No answer. He hit the bell again and again.

"Honey, calm down," Chantal whispered.

Finally, the back door opened and Pete stepped out, Pepsi in hand.

"Pete, I need to use your telescope again."

"Hello Damian. It's overcast, you won't see anything today."

"I don't care. I'll give it a try."

"It only works once, Damian. Lots of people come back and they want to use the telescope again. They want a second chance. But my policy is - no second chances."

"What the fuck."

"Damian. No profanity. Please; we had a nice time together. Let's not spoil it." With a quizzical look on his pudgy face, Pete picked up the little silver bell in his hand and retreated to the back room. Before he closed the varnished door, he asked in a plain tone of voice. "You seem upset. Did something happen?"

The 21 Mine

Chantal took Damian's hand and tried to pull him away from the front desk. At first he flung her hand away and simply put his head down in his folded arms on the top of the desk. He wanted to cry.

"I should have gone back to Harlem," he muttered.

"Don't say that. Let's go. Pete's always been a little strange. Come on."

* * * *

"Come on, let's cross the street. We're going to the Palace like we planned." Damian took a deep breath, raising and lowering his chest. Finally, in resignation, he said, "I don't know what I could have done differently, I guess."

Fu Zin, the owner of Golden Palace, had just finished his morning game of mahjong, the only time he relaxed each day, when the phone rang. It was the Chinese-American lawyer from Chinatown. As he listened, Zin's face turned pale. He hung up and turned to his new, young, Chinese wife, Ming Lee.

"They want to know if Klocks is really dead. They want me to hire two more who crossed the border at Akwesasne. I don't want to do business with these snakeheads."

His wife erupted in a burst of excited Fukienese dialect that even most Chinese couldn't understand. She was obviously upset. When she spit out the words Hong Kong, her husband got even more rattled, and that's when the first customers of the day tromped up the sidewalk on Broad Street. She recognized Damian and knew Chantal and, when they walked in, Ming Lee plastered a smile on her face.

"Good morning, how are you?" Ming Lee said. Fu Zin moved back to the giant wok and switched on the exhaust fan, not wanting to be with customers just yet, particularly this black Damian fellow. He just didn't trust him, and wasn't convinced that his escaped prison friend was dead.

"Fair to middling," Chantal said, not in a mood to hide her disgust at their recent turn of events.

Chantal and Damian ordered Chinese vegetables and rice and wonton soup. They both just picked at their meal with their chopsticks and stared across the street at Jimmy's and the newspapers. Damian stood up, fished in his pocket for some quarters and walked across Broad Street to buy the Plattsburgh Press Republican.

The story was still on the front page, but no longer on top. The headline was 'Search For Escaped Inmate Called Off.' Damian read the lead paragraph to Chantal. 'Mineville - Authorities have called off their search for Wallace Klocks, a Moriah Shock Incarceration Facility inmate who escaped Friday and is feared dead inside a nearby mine shaft.'

Damian rolled his eyes and continued reading. ' "In more than 48 hours of searching the 21 pit we have found no further sign, other than Klocks' tracks and his right boot, leading into this dangerous underground maze," said Warden Adiaz DeJesus. He added that searchers "have found no sign that Klocks made his way out. It is my belief that the inmate is hopelessly lost or drowned, inside those mines." '

"Get this," Damian said, skipping to the last three lines which he read aloud. 'Wallace Klocks was sentenced to one to four years for burglary. He would have been eligible for parole June 1st. Klocks was to testify next week in Albany in a separate federal case.'

"Another case. Yeah, why don't they tell us more about the other case?" Damian looked past the girl to Fu Zin, while Chantal held his forearm, trying to comfort him.

"Stop. Damian, there's nothing you can do and anything you do will just make things worse."

Damian collected himself and sat there dejected. "It's amazing he made it. All the guy eats are cookies and oatmeal. You watch, he'll start bugging you for cookies. Peanut butter cookies. Chocolate-chip cookies."

"I have a couple of new ingredients I could put in vanilla and, let me see, arsenic."

twenty two

Klocks awoke hungry and dirty. He showered in the cold singing, "Singing in the Rain." It was one of the happiest days of his life. Damian and Chantal returned from town and their early Chinese lunch, still unsure about what to do - now that they were harboring an escaped con. Chantal walked into the ranch house. Damian knew his place as a ranch hand and never entered unless he was invited by the old lady, the mistress of the brood. So far, he had enjoyed three dinners there.

Damian shoved open the bunkhouse door, and there stood Wallace Klocks, butt naked, stark white, muscular and ropy with a slight hunch to his shoulders.

"If I was still inside, I wouldn't be walking around like this, you know that," Klocks said toweling off his hair while he examined his surroundings. "Just about the same size as my last cell, but more wood and less metal. Funny, sometimes it's all in your head. That's how guys do years and years of time. They convince themselves they like it, being taken care of, and then, lo and behold, they do like it."

"The woman thing. I know guys on the outside who don't get laid in a year, and don't care either, and they're not queer. You know they just have other priorities. They're at the track all the time, or they like to work and drink, and that's it."

Damian tossed the paper on the lower bunk. "You're in there Klocks, only you're lost in the mines."

Still naked, Klocks picked up the paper, and stood with his back against an exposed stud next to the light of a window. He concentrated, and Damian watched him pronounce each word in a whisper to himself as he read about the search being called off.

"They think I'm dead. If I did drugs, or smoked, or ate beef, I'd be dead. It was my conditioning and will that got me through. Yeah, I knew they'd hate that place. They think I'm down there in my tomb. Man, that's perfect." Klocks rolled the paper up and tossed it at Damian, while allowing himself a big grin. "You got some pants, blue jeans or something, punk?"

"Sure, Klocks, take the clothes off my back. Yeah, I got a pair of blue jeans, here, they're going to be a little big."

Damian took them off the closet hook and tossed them to Klocks.

"Thanks buddy, we're in this together."

"Yeah, unfortunately I see that. Why did you run? Man, you only had three weeks left."

Ordinarily, Klocks didn't answer questions like that, but he was in a contemplative, philosophical mood. Rubbing his unshaved chin between his thumb and forefinger, he gave it some thought.

"I was caught. Caught between the cops and the crooks. The only reason I'm not in Dannemora is I turned state's evidence on a smuggling case. I got involved and I knew who was running the show, at least here in the States."

"What were you smuggling?"

"Listen kid, I tell you about my work, and then you're in trouble. Then you can hurt me. But what happens is I don't trust anybody, not a girl I've been fucking, not a guy I've been pulling heists with. And then I hurt the other guy first out of my own fear. So you don't want to know. Because then I know you can harm me. And I know when cops are offering time off your sentence for a little information about me, you'll give it up, you'll rat. How do I know that, because I've given more information on more crooks to more cops than you'll ever know. That's why I'm in minimum, instead of in Dannemora."

"But you know what? I'll tell you anyway, because in this case I was a plant from the start. What were we smuggling? We were smuggling people, over the border down from Canada, Chinese immigrants, by the hundreds, through the

The 21 Mine

St. Regis reservation, at Akwesasne, and through the dozens of unmanned trails and dirt roads up there in the woods. Big business, lots of money. Twenty to fifty thousand dollars per Chinese, per alien. And I fingered the boss. Would you believe it? A Chinese-American lawyer in Chinatown. A woman. A woman who would just as soon kill me as kill a cockroach. Once she knew I was going to testify against her, I was dead. No question. The Chinese always work together. They're always in debt to the big boss. And in this operation she was the big boss. There would be a slant eye after a slant eye after me for the rest of my life. And what did the investigator tell me would happen if I didn't testify? I was back to Dannemora and they were bringing up a murder charge against me. I wasn't going back to max, to serve out a life sentence, no way. So, shit, I did what I do best, I escaped. And now I'm in control of me. I'm the captain of me."

Damian was silent, mesmerized by so much talk out of a guy who usually said so little.

"Now Damian, these blue jeans are too long. Give me your knife."

As Klocks was cutting two inches off the bottom, he looked up to Damian. "I see you got a hold of Billy's nail gun. Never know. Might come in handy. Damian, I'm going to need some money. The sooner I can get some money, the sooner I can get out of here and out of your hair."

Damian was feeling trapped, lured once again into trouble.

Klocks put down the knife and picked up the paper. Damian took the opportunity to close the Puma knife and slide it back into his pocket. Klocks caught the movement, and was going to make Damian give the knife up, but he let it go.

"Shit, couldn't have worked out better. I knew they'd hate it down there. Too fucking dangerous. Too fucking cold and wet. Perfect place. Perfect article. . . and I had the strength, the discipline, the will, to do it right. Thank you, all mighty Klocks."

For a second, Klocks contemplated Damian. "You got any ideas, young Damian?"

"Klocks, you dropped out of the sky, you gotta to know that. I mean coming up out of the earth, that's spooky."

"I am spooky and I need money." He looked vacantly at the wood stove without really seeing it. "Are there any gas stations around?"

"Yeah, there's a Stewart's down in Port Henry. That's where Chantal goes anyway."

"I'd hang around too, if I was tight with her. But I got plans. I got a reputation to uphold. You know, after you're gone, what else do you have? I want to be remembered. Billy the Kidd, Jesse James, Son of Sam, Wallace the Rock Klocks, Wallace the Owl Klocks. Hoo hoo, boo hoo. Oxilating, dododo." Klocks, the mercurial one, was strumming the air guitar a` la Jimi Hendrix, dancing around in Damian's blue jeans.

"So, I guess you get happy if you make it. Pulling off a stunt like this, that's something," Damian said as he tossed Klocks one of his Tommy Hilfiger T-shirts.

Klocks held up the shirt to check it out. "That's not me. I'm not in the ghetto now. You got a wool shirt. Haven't you ever seen what the guards wear before they change. Blue jeans and a wool shirt. But I guess blending in isn't something you can do, is it?"

"Klocks, you don't understand. I don't want trouble. I got a good thing here with Chantal. I just fell into it. I'll help you. But nothing illegal."

"You didn't call the cops, so you already helped me. And you and I know, I'm not going down easy. You call the cops and you're going down hard."

Damian knew his predicament. Damian wasn't going to rat on anybody, but he didn't like getting sucked into Klocks' crooked plans, bizarre and unpredictable. "Klocks, I got news for you. There are no cops in Port Henry. There are no cops in Moriah, except the guards at the prison. If you call the cops, Chantal said you call state police in Westport, twenty miles and a good half hour drive away."

"Good. Now, tell me about the gas station."

"It's a chain, with like a mini-mart inside."

"Do they pump a lot of gas?"

"Yep. Everybody goes there, old and young."

"Okay, that means lots of cash. Now we just got to find out what they do with it every night."

The 21 Mine

Klocks eyed Damian in a peculiar fashion. "You're staying here right? As long as you're poking that woman Chantal, right? You got to find a job, don't you? Fast service places are always looking for part-timers, guys to work Friday and Saturday nights. There's your job."

Damian was panicking at what he saw ahead. "Everyone knows I was in Moriah Shock. They're not going to hire me."

"Yeah, they're going to hire you. Because if they don't they're discriminating against your black ass."

Damian put his hands on his hips. "Isn't that just peachy. And once they hire me, let me guess. You break in the gas station, with a little help from an ex-con on the inside. Great."

"Yeah, so what. It's part of a chain, this Stewart's. They have insurance. They budget for this kind of thing. And you just told me there's no cops here anyway, so I'm not going to get caught. And once I get the cash, I'm long gone. Maybe I'll give you a couple of hundred. Damian, my man. Relax, I'm untouchable, you're talking to a ghost."

"A ghost. Well, Chantal saw this ghost too."

"Son, do you have some control over your new found love? Because, since I'm in such a mood for yapping, I'll tell you something. No one has ever squealed on me and lived. That's right, and lived. Even the suspicion that someone might turn me in, gnaws on my brain until I relieve the pressure and eliminate the person. So Damian, buddy, I leave it up to you to convince me that Chantal will leave me be as Casper the Friendly Ghost. I'm warning you now. That's what you want, you want me as Casper."

Damian was getting nervous with Klocks' neurotic chatter as Klocks was walking in circles now, his fists clenched, repeating that he was "Casper the friendly, I say friendly, ghost!"

"Klocks, I will talk to Chantal. But the last thing you want is attention. You're a free man now, don't screw it up. You disappear into the mountains or the city and you're a new man. Remember, you won. They think you're dead."

Damian felt for once he had stood up to Klocks, the seasoned, callused, loner whom everyone gave space to, because they knew he was connected and he was cruel. Tied to the detectives, hardly ever doing time, and diabolic the way he could turn for the sake of saving himself and nailing somebody else.

"Damian. Last favor. This is it, then I'm history. You'll be clean. I'll be gone. Help me out here. Jesus, I just crawled my way out of a maze of death."

twenty three

Klocks, who never smoked before, was now smoking Camels. Ever since he had confined himself to the bunkhouse and the fields leading to the forest. The next evening, as the stars first shone, he was drawn back to the aspen trees in the middle of the paddock. He sat on the rock above the hole in the ground that had saved his life. For a moment he pondered if it was just him that had saved himself. Was he lucky or was there something more? The cool breeze on the hairs of legs let him know he was alive and for some reason evoked his childhood memories of running away up to Prospect Park in Troy where he'd sit on the overlook and watch the city sparkle below and beyond him. He remembered the city looking like a twinkling fairyland. But he knew Troy close-up too, so the dream had died.

Now the stars, first Vega, then the North Star, and then the Big Dipper, part of the Great Bear constellation, twinkled to him, and since he knew nothing of them close-up, they were one hundred percent beautiful and the dream lingered.

Klocks' favorite constellation was Canis Minor, the lesser dog. He didn't know why, maybe because of the mutt that used to follow him around as a kid on First Avenue. He had called him Minor and fed him sugar doughnuts from Dunkin Donuts.

The beauty lingered because there were no people beneath the woods here in the night sky. No people to betray him. No little kids without dads. He tried to shut that thought out. It had been haunting him. Detective Wesley, who had cut his sentence in return for giving it up on others criminals, was hunting him, trying to push his buttons, pressuring him about a boy who would never see his father. A father that knew too much about Klocks' professional activities. How did the cop know that not hurting kids was one of his mantras, one of Klocks' soft spots?

Klocks didn't know how long he was out there on the rock. After he saw one shooting star, he left and walked back through the paddock, easily squeezing between the second and third rails in the fence, following the dirt path back to the bunkhouse.

Klocks took a last drag on the Camel, and stuffed the butt through the pop-top opening of a can of Pepsi. He lit one of the old candle stubs that lined the window sill next to the moths. He went to grab another of Freihofer's fruit cookies, but he had eaten them all. "I'm stronger than those," he said out loud pointing to the pack of Camels. "But I can't stay here much longer. I need something to do. Play poker or something." Klocks dangled his legs off the bunk, staring vacantly, his mind back in the center of the paddock, with the breeze from the light hole below and the twinkle and glow of the stars above, where for a moment he felt maybe there was a God, something bigger than antiques and making money.

Damian slowly pushed open the bunkhouse door, resentful that what was once his hideaway, his love nest, was now Klocks' place. Damian noticed the lit candle. "I asked you to wait until I got back."

"Hey, where's my ice cream."

"You don't like ice cream, remember, it's fattening and you're a hard ass."

"Yeah, but there's not a hell of a lot else going on up here." Klocks didn't miss a beat from his prior soliloquy and delivered his closing monologue directly to Damian. "Hell, if I had died in those mines, I would have been one of many. Just the first convict among miners, that's all. But it wasn't to be, was it?"

"No, it wasn't to be." Damian said while mulling over his own torn allegiance.

"There's lots you don't know, Damian. And you know what, that's why I like you. I'll tell you something. You know Spike, the guard? We go way back. Way back. We both grew up on the south side of Troy, on First Avenue.

The 21 Mine

Damian wasn't totally surprised by the information, remembering the sly way Spike had mentioned Klocks.

"Still Klocks, you could walk away."

"Yeah, but I got things on my brain, things bugging me. Things you don't know about. I got the Chinese and I got a detective buzzing around my hive. The Chinese clan won't let go. I don't know, all of a sudden up here in the woods, I'm feeling lonely. I've always been alone, but never lonely. Maybe It's the goddamn stars. They're giving me religion. I never saw them in prison, the lights were so bright."

* * * *

"You remember Randy?" Klocks asked.

"Yeah, of course," Damian said, waiting for the rest of the story.

"Well, before I escaped, strike that, before I disappeared and died," he smirked, "we talked. He said there's this place down in Florida, not too far from Havana and those fence posts - a place called Apalachicola. It's a peninsula on the Panhandle. Beaches, great seafood. Do you like oysters? Man, their oysters are the best. I mean you know oysters. You know what they remind me of."

"Yeah, I know what they remind you of; now get to the point."

"Easy brother, not so fast," Klocks said, eyeing Damian, wondering where he came up with this new found attitude. Maybe prison had toughened him up. "The point is that's where I want to head. Randy said the cops don't bother you and it's out of the way," and then changing his voice and mocking himself, "a little off the beaten track, as they say."

"I've never been there, and I'm not sure I want to go there. Things are good for me here."

"What, you're going to stay another winter up here? Might as well be back in prison - except for the pussy." Klocks glanced around at the bunkhouse. "The accommodations are better in the slammer."

"Why don't you leave the country? Go to Canada. Chantal and I are talking about driving to Montreal for the weekend."

"First of all, I don't want to cross the frigging border. I don't have a passport. And if I did, what am I going to do; hand them my Wallace Klocks passport? 'Oh yeah, you're the guy that drowned in the mines. I read about you. But they never found your body. Drive right on through. Enjoy your vacation.'"

"The way if figure it," Klocks continued, "you can drive right to Florida, no hassles. No border to cross. No I.D. to fake. Randy says he used to camp on some place called Alligator Point. Beautiful sandy beaches, Florida State coeds. They'd love you down there."

"I.D.s are your problem, man. I'm all properly discharged. I still got my driver's license and guess what, it hasn't expired. And just to tell you, Chantal says you don't need a passport to get across the border. Sometimes they don't ask you for nothing."

"I'd guess they'd ask us, wouldn't they. You don't think they'd ask a black guy with a white girl?"

"Klocks . . "

"It's Deed, I told you, it's Deed."

"All right Deed, you're behind the times. You still have that paranoid prison mentality. But then you escaped, didn't you, and I was released, wasn't I?" Damian saw he had pushed it as far as he dared, and shut up. He knew who he was messing with. But he also knew that at this time, in this bunkhouse, Klocks either had to embrace him or . . . or kill him. And Damian hadn't pegged Klocks as a killer.

"What? You're going to stay around here. Is that what you're going to do? You don't have any money, and I'll tell you, once the snow flies you'll wish you were gone. Look, Damian, I need your help, okay? I don't want to stay here and I can't stay here. There's Spike, there's the Chinese, there's the prison. Man, if I stuck around, I know I'd slip up, they'd find out. All I'm asking you is to think about it."

Damian had never heard him be sincere like this, and he buckled. "All right, I'll think about it."

"Think about leaving with me?"

"No way, Jose. I'll think about leaving here with Chantal, and if we can help you. . ." He stopped. "I don't know Klocks. I just want to be done with it. I want out."

"So do I. So do I."

"Yes Klocks, but you and I are different. This is your total life, man. This isn't my life and I don't want to make it my life. I was sent here for smoking pot."

"For selling pot," Klocks corrected him.

"Whatever. I got sent here for diddly-squat. The hicks around here smoke pot. Chantal smokes pot. Her mom smokes pot."

Klocks calmed himself and cleared his head. He sensed a crack in Damian's armor, and since he had learned that Damian actually had a license, he was even more intent on winning him over. Klocks stood up, drawn to the window by a far-away series of low, sonorous hoots.

He put his finger to his mouth and froze. "Hear that."

"No," Damian said dryly.

"Well listen, you ignorant son of a bitch." They observed a moment of tense silence. "There. Hoo, hoo-hoo," Klocks mimicked. He gestured intently." That's the hoot of a Great Horned Owl. If that isn't a sign, I don't know what is."

"Yes, it's an omen," Damian parroted, telling Klocks what he wanted to hear.

"I have to admit that now that the snow's gone it's all nature here," Klocks said calmly. And now he played his king. "I've got some money. In Troy. Five thousand dollars. I need someone to go pick it up for me," and his ace, "so I can buy a car."

It was an obvious purchase, in a way, unless he was going to take a train or fly to Florida, to Apalachicola. Certainly driving was the most anonymous way of getting there. But until this conversation with Damian, he hadn't thought of it. It might have been luck, or it might have been Klocks' transcendence, but Klocks had hit upon Damian's one desire, to buy a car, to buy a very specific car, a baby-blue Cadillac convertible.

Now the wheels turned in Damian's head the way the wheels always turned in Klocks' head. Maneuvering, thinking what's in it for him, but not realizing that Klocks' peculiar sphere of influence, calculated or not, had stumbled upon Damian's Achilles.

"I bet you don't have a license," Damian ventured, feigning assurance.

"You bet right," Klocks said.

Damian started to see the jam Klocks was in. No records, no car, no registration, no purchase of sale could ever have Klocks' real name on it. Not around here. Not this year. As for this name, Deed, he'd need a fake driver's license and a raft of phony I.Ds.

"What kind of car are you going to buy?" Damian asked.

"I don't know. What kind of car do you want?" Klocks shot back.

With the silence that followed, Klocks knew he had him. 'My gift,' he said to himself.

"I'll need someone to go down to Troy and pick up the money," Klocks began, already making the assumption that Damian had agreed to his final plan. Damian had swallowed the bait like it was a tasty Apalachicola oyster.

"Whoa, how are you going to buy a car?"

Klocks knew that was coming. "That's where you come in. You buy the car. You get me to Apalachicola. It's your car."

"I got to talk to Chantal," Damian said and walked out the door. In the dark on his on his way to the main house, he heard a chilling hoo hoo, the second and third hoots of the Great Horned Owl.

twenty four

The next morning, after Damian's futile attempt for a nighttime confab, Chantal grabbed him by the hand and led him into the woods. They both knew it wasn't to make love. They were on the other side of the ranch property, having been displaced by Casper the ghost at the bunkhouse. Chantal was leading Damian to the flat rock where, as a girl, she used to lay out and catch the rays. It had to be windy, otherwise the blackflies drove her back inside. This was a billowy, day, and she and her boyfriend needed to get away and talk.

Damian didn't say a word as Chantal led him through a thicket of blue spruce that itched him every time he brushed a branch. After a stretch of climbing, they came upon a clearing of tall rye grass. The sun shone on a flat outcropping of granite by an oak tree at the top edge of the secluded field, where they stopped and took in the modest view.

"There's the prison," Damian remarked sullenly.

"Our family still refers to it as the Fisher Hill Mine," Chantal said proudly. "Sit down, Damian. I used to come here as a girl, to be alone."

Damian was happy just to sit down and hang out, just to let the day slide by like he used to do on summer days in Harlem.

She sat next to him, shuffling some loose stone away with her cowboy boots to make a place for herself. On the horizon to the northwest toward the High Peaks, a large bird soared, probably a turkey vulture above the Westport dump. With the vulture's keen vision, Chantal thought, the two of us are clearly visible on this flat rock in the northern forest.

Damian put his arm around her and halfheartedly asked, "What's up?"

"What is up?" she repeated, loudly, enunciating each syllable in contrast to Damian's slurred 'S'up?' "You know what's up. Klocks is out to get you." She paused before she went on, flicking an acorn down the slope into the blowing field. "I've risked a lot teaming up with you. I'm sure a lot of people are talking. I know my mother's not happy. I don't want to prove them all right. If we team up with Klocks." Then she stopped to rephrase. "If you team up with Klocks, you're going back to that prison over there," she said flicking another acorn in the direction of a long building of squad bays, "and you're losing me. I'm not getting involved with that guy. He's a professional crook and he'll take us all down. Damian, look at me."

"Now you sound like my mother," Damian said, rolling his head, feeling sorry for himself. "You don't understand, in prison you have to have a few buddies, you got to stick together. There's no stronger bond. After Klocks and I fought, Well, after he kicked my butt, he kind of looked after me. I don't know why. But nobody messed with me, because they knew Klocks and I were tight. I can't just walk away from him now. "

"You can't?" Chantal asked. "Can you walk away from me? Because that's your choice, Damian, my friend, that's your choice. If it wasn't for me, you and your wishy-washy head would be back on the streets of Harlem getting into trouble."

"As opposed to up here doing what? " Damian asked.

"You can get a job. I can help you get a job," Chantal said with a hint of pleading in her voice.

"You and Klocks. You both have a job lined up for me. He wants me to work at Stewart's."

"Stewart's. Why Stewart's? she asked with a perplexed look on her face. "That would have been one of my suggestions. I know the manager."

"Okay, let's back up a little, sister." Damian looked around at the kind of nature he had only seen in books. "It is pretty here, and so are you."

"Please, Damian. This is serious."

"Is it amazing or what?" he said, more as a statement than a question.

"Is what amazing?" she asked.

"Klocks' escape. It's the most amazing thing I've ever seen. I mean come on. He's successfully disappeared off the face of the earth. He's free."

"Look, honey. Yes, the escape itself is hard to believe. It's amazing. You're right, it's amazing. But free, I don't think so. He can't go anywhere. He can't do anything. He can't buy anything. That's why he needs you. Now, you've talked to me about that Cadillac. That's your dream. And if you throw that away, if you hand that to him, your dream, then you're not a man. Not my man anyway."

She stopped talking. They both leaned back on the rock, and Damian rolled over and buried his head in her shoulder. She was getting to him. If he was going to do this, really stand up to Klocks, he saw that he needed her, that he couldn't do it without her.

Damian started to daydream he was playing basketball on the court outside P.S. 154. He was good. Someone passed to him. He passed back. Life was easy then. Now there were these strong characters to deal with.

He snapped back. "Let's talk about us for a minute," Damian said. "What if Casper had never popped up from behind that rock, like a ghost from behind a tombstone?" Damian was shaking his head in disbelief. "What if it was just us. What would we be doing, you and I?" he asked in a challenging fashion.

"You and I? We'd be having fun," she said with a touch of uncertainty.

"Yeah, but then what?" he asked pointedly, sitting up and moving away from her, flicking a bit of moss off his blue jeans.

"You mean, are we going to be together long term?"

"That's part of the question."

"Well, I can't answer that. I like being with you. I'm not married, you're not married. Not that I'm aiming for that," she noted quickly.

"What are you aiming for?"

Finally, she got her dander up again. "Damian, why are you grilling me?" Now, she too was standing up. "Klocks is the culprit, here, not me."

"Chantal, I know that. But I want to know if you're with me for the long haul."

"Damian, honey, I'm with you. But you're twenty-two and I'm thirty-four. You're from the city and I'm from the country. And you're black and I'm white."

"You left out one thing. You're a woman and I'm a man. And we're supposed to be different," he said leaning into her, tilting forward.

"Yeah," she started giggling, "but not that different." Damian saw the humor there too, and they stood together, hugging and swaying on the flat rock. One thing Chantal recognized, but wouldn't verbalize, was that she liked the action, the intrigue. Her two weeks since she had met Damian had been the most exciting two weeks she'd ever experienced in Essex County, that's for sure.

"Damian, sweetie. Look, we've got to go. But a couple of quick practical things. Take the job at Stewart's. I know that sounds crazy, coming from me. But it's a job you can do. Like I said, I can talk to the manager. And that's how you stand up to Klocks. Not by fighting him, God forbid. But by taking the job, staying honest, and not doing his bidding. Be a working stiff, buy into this community. Hey, you stay here long enough you could be the mayor.

"Not likely," Damian said.

"No, you're right, not likely."

"Are we leaving?" Damian asked.

"Yes, I told Heidi I'd have Brushstrokes ready for the show this weekend and you have to clean the stalls. Remember, you're still working here."

They had talked themselves out, but felt closer for it and wound their way back to the ranch. Damian took one last look over his shoulder at the prison tower, his view blurred by the tall pines. He was not quite far enough away yet to gain any clear perspective. As for the days ahead, he had faith they'd work themselves out, and with the help of Hurricane, he was mostly right.

twenty five

Spike lumbered into the Golden Palace and sat down for his late night snack. His shift was over and things at the prison had finally calmed down, now that Klocks was gone. Spike noticed a new worker behind the counter. Well, new to all of Port Henry, except Spike. It was Funny Fungi, the same Fungi Klocks had drop-kicked up at Moriah Shock. He was released at the same time as Damian.

Fungi came around the counter to the small sitting area and bowed slightly to Spike. "Mr. Hurricane, so pleased to see you again. More pleasant surroundings, don't you agree?"

"Things don't change much, eh Fungi?" Spike said in a derisive tone. "You're still in the kitchen."

"Yes, Mr. Hurricane, but our friend isn't around, right?"

Spike looked up from the menu suspiciously. He was the only customer.

"I'm ready to order," Spike said. "I'll take the Kung Po Chicken. Or is it Kung Fu?" Spike chuckled. "How's your hearing, by the way?"

"My hearing is fine," Fungi responded, instinctively touching his cauliflower ear, but refusing to be rattled by Spike's nasty sense of humor. Fungi turned and looked to the back of the kitchen where the boss, Fu Zin, was on the phone. After an exchange of meaningful glances, Fu Zin nodded an emphatic yes to Fungi.

Fungi looked outside to the darkened streets of Broad and Main. On a weekday night at 11:00, no one was out. Mustering some courage, and at the behest of his higher-ups, Fungi sat down opposite Spike.

"Mr. Hurricane, I must speak to you."

"I see that, Fungi," Spike said, spreading out his legs and crossing his arms, then leaning back in his chair so that he took up about three times the space of Fungi.

"You know Damian, the inmate. He was released with me."

"Yeah, onward, of course I know the creep."

"Well, maybe he and his friend, his girlfriend, think we no speak English, but we all speak English, and we all have good ears, except for one ear," he said smiling and pointing to the side of his head away from Spike. "They talk a lot. We think Klocks is alive."

"No kidding," Spike said feigning surprise, and covering up his own uncertainty.

"We," he said gesturing with his head back to the kitchen, where Fu Zin and his wife Ming Lee were now clearly watching their conversation. "We happy with Klocks now. Everything's fine. Case dismissed!" Fungi said laughing.

Fungi continued laughing as Fu Zin and Ming Lee walked from the back of the kitchen around the counter by them to the front door. Fu Zin reached in his pocket for a key and as he turned the lock, he bobbed his head at Spike and said, "It's late; that's all. No need for interruption."

Quickly assessing the situation, Spike brought the chair upright, and uncrossed his arms. If he had to, he figured he could toss two of them through the plate glass window, and claim they were retaliating for something he had done in prison to Fungi.

Now Fu Zin took over. "Here's the situation. If Klocks is alive, it's good for him, for sure, and good for us too. Bad for us only if he's still around here. He helped us, now we want to help him. You know this is a cash business," he said waving his hand at the row of pictures of the various Chinese dishes hanging above the counter, "and tonight we have extra cash. And we want you to have some. We're just giving it to you, let's say, for saving Fungi in prison, and let's say just for eating here all these late nights."

The 21 Mine

Fu Zin slid a stack of bills halfway across the table.

Spike looked around quizzically. "I have to go to the little boy's room," he said, tossing his napkin over the money, and walking the ten feet to the single, large bathroom.

When Spike emerged and sat down again, he grabbed his napkin and put it in his lap like a good boy. "Now where were we?" he asked.

Ming Lee had left the discussion and was in the back, on the phone. In his alert state, Spike listened as she keyed in an eleven digit number. Probably calling Chinatown, he thought.

"Now," Fu Zin continued, his hands clasped together in front of him, his mouth turned down with internal apprehension, "we want you to find Klocks and take him away. Better for him, better for us. We think this black fellow Damian is the linchpin." he said, happy with his choice of words.

To confirm Fu Zin's brilliance, Spike said, "Yes, you think he's the key, very good. All of you really do speak English."

"You help him leave, and another napkin will fall in your lap." They had finished their offering and were patiently waiting for some type of indication from Spike. Ming Lee remained on the phone, presumably to the female lawyer representing the Fukienese in Chinatown. Fungi with the prison background, and Fu Zin who had implicitly or otherwise worked with Spike before waited with crooked smiles. The Chinese might become a problem, Spike's problem. He didn't know what evidence lay where. Really, his only involvement in the smuggling business had been to shut up. So this offer was hard to refuse. Plus, he needed money to repair some waterline rot on the transom of his prized boat, and the only repair place was down in Lake George. He looked outside. No witnesses. His word against the Chinese. And finally, he secretly hoped Klocks was still alive. Though Klocks was ruthless, coming from the gutter in Troy, the way he did, Spike saw a perverse nobility in the Owl..

Spike stood up and glared at the tiny Chinese, who sat up straight in rigid nervousness. Then Spike flashed his Cheshire cat grin, and bowed slightly, mimicking the Chinese. "At your service."

Fu Zin smiled, and nodded back to his wife on the phone, while Funny Fungi laughed nervously. "One request though," Spike said. "If by some miracle,

Klocks is alive and still around here, and if somehow I convince him to leave, I get free Chinese here for the next decade."

"Free food," Fu Zin repeated with a sour face. With that the Chinese engaged in a heated five minute discussion, gesturing and arguing back and forth with Ming Lee who was now off the phone.

Finally, Fungi and Fu Zin stood up, sizing up Spike like a big steak, possibly trying to envision how much he really could eat.

To himself Spike was saying, make me you an offer, you idiots. Haven't you ever heard of negotiating?

They must have read his mind. Ming Lee called out, "Once a week, free, that's it."

"Fine," Spike said. Before he stepped out the door, he thought for a moment. "That second napkin, if there's anything to this, I'll need it before I complete the job. You don't know Klocks. He bargains hard, and things could get messy."

Spike pulled on the door and the plate glass next to it vibrated with the force of his tug. Fu Zin raced over and unlocked the door, and Spike disappeared around the corner.

twenty six

It was Tuesday, his day off. Spike tossed his shotgun on the back seat as if it were duck hunting season. Only it wasn't, which is why he didn't put the shotgun in the rack where it would be visible. He drove his Bronco out of the village of Westport up the Stevenson Road, the back way to Port Henry. Only then he turned up Mountain Spring Road and drove for five or six miles up past Bartlett Pond through the woods beyond the last scattering of summer camps, until the road was a rutted washboard full of weeds that simply ended in an overgrown field. He hadn't seen a car or a person since he turned off Stevenson. He parked where the remnants of the road stopped. He had about a half mile walk through the woods until he reached Cook Shaft Road, which separated the backside of Moriah Shock from Heidi's ranch.

Spike had dated Chantal when she was more innocent and less savvy. He had been drawn to the bevy of girls at Heidi's Bog Pond Ranch, just like a lot of other young Adirondack men. Finding Klocks was easy. Spike knew the ranch, had hunted deer nearby in the hills of Witherbee and Mineville. He knew all too well that Damian was staying there, and now he had an opportunity to confirm Damian's presence.

He took a last look in his Bronco. He had put an extra two gallon tank of gas in the back for his Hacker Craft. When he picked up his shotgun, he felt through the rip inside the seat where he had wedged in the second napkin of money. He knew on a Tuesday in the spring not a soul would be at Velez's

179

marina. Spike was always the first one with his boat in the water, the classiest wooden boat this side of Vermont. Most of Spike's spending cash went toward that wooden boat. He had already arranged for somebody, another old and dear friend from Troy, to pick up his boat south of Fort Ticonderoga and trailer it the few miles to Black Point Road and the state boat-launching site at Mossy Point. From there, he would slip into Lake George and motor across for repairs at the Hacker Boat Company in Silver Bay.

It was a beautiful day and Spike enjoyed the hike having convinced himself that he had done nothing wrong, nor did he plan to. But with each step closer doubt crept in. He hadn't been alone, face to face with Klocks, outside of Moriah Shock, in years. It might be more emotional than he counted on, especially if Klocks didn't see the wisdom of what he had planned.

As he made his way by Bartlett Pond, swatting mosquitoes, a gaggle of geese swept down on the pond. Wouldn't you know it. That never happened when he was out there freezing in the blind pretending he was a bunch of reeds.

Spike let out a guffaw. Even as a kid, he was big, and Klocks was small. For a while as kids in Troy they were close pals. Spike was the brawn and Klocks was the brain. Sometimes, Spike would go terrorizing around the neighborhood carrying Klocks up on his shoulders. That's why the two of them loved the character Master-Blaster in the movie Beyond Thunder Dome. But they had gone their separate ways, Spike abetting his size with some mental savvy and Klocks supplementing his cerebral gifts by becoming a lethal physical specimen. And now twenty years later, they met again, in prison, both smart enough not to let on that they knew the other. Nothing to be gained by making it public.

By now, Spike could see the sunlight reflecting off the silvery razor wire atop the back fence, still impressed that Klocks had climbed over without shredding himself. He veered away from the prison to Heidi's property. He had done his homework and knew Damian was staying in the bunkhouse. His heartbeat increased.

Damian would be a piece of cake. Klocks, if he was really alive and depending on his mood, was another matter. He had a mean streak. A cruel side to him. The same side that had helped him survive thus far, Spike thought, trying to give his old First Avenue friend the benefit of the doubt.

Spike headed through the woods, dense with an undergrowth of poplars - probably logged six years ago, Spike guessed. From the edge of Heidi's property, the bunkhouse was clearly visible. Spike was sweating under his long sleeve shirt, but he liked to sweat, and then drink beer afterwards. Spike judged by the sun that it was about noon. If all went according to plan, he had a long day, and some key stops, ahead of him. He wasn't sure what to do with the shotgun, how to play it.

There was nothing but open field between him and the bunkhouse. He spied a few horses in the shade of the aspens near the boulder in the center of the large paddock. Probably the one Billy and his crew had built. Spike didn't dwell on it too long. He really had no choice but to walk directly across the field outside the paddock. Nobody else was around. No purple king-cab was parked near the barn. The clan was probably having lunch in the main house or even in town.

Spike walked casually but directly to the bunkhouse, coming at it from the side. Before stepping up onto the wooden deck which was sure to creak, he carefully placed the shotgun around the corner in the grass, barrel down, safety off, leaning up against the side of the bunkhouse.

Spike didn't know it yet, but Klocks was there, inside, stretched out on the lower bunk in his shorts, waiting for Damian to come back from town with his decision about helping him out. Klocks had lied to him on one issue. There was no money in Troy. But Klocks needed Damian's help, and he was getting restless. The money was just a carrot from one crook to another. That's the way Klocks viewed it. He had completely recuperated from his ordeal of a week ago, and, according to Damian, even the rumors and talk in town were subsiding. Klocks held a map of Florida in his hand, and for the umpteenth time, turned it sideways to get a better look at the Florida Panhandle. He was ready for action, tired of waiting.

Spike actually considered knocking, but instead pushed the door open with his foot. Klocks lowered the map, which was falling apart at the creases. Spike's frame filled the entire doorway, the sunlight outlining his body, momentarily blinding Klocks. His instinct was to reach for the nail gun, but he quickly reverted to reptilian mode and remained perfectly still staring at this outline of a hulk at the door.

Almost meekly, Spike spoke. "It's me, Spike."

Klocks didn't respond and didn't move.

Spike was thrown off. "It's me, Spike . . . Hurricane."

Klocks slowly brought up both hands to shield his eyes, raising himself partially up as if he were doing crunches. "It is you. You son of a bitch. You goddamn fool. You know you shouldn't be here."

"Shouldn't be here. You're the one that shouldn't be here. You're dead, remember."

Klocks was standing now, the map having fallen to the floor next to a worn paperback. "Are you alone?"

"Yep, came in through the woods."

"Spiiikeeee!" Klocks screamed and with head down charged the big fellow, tackling him, sending him backwards out onto the deck. And once he was on him, kissed him all over on the top of the head. "Spiiikeeee!" Klocks screamed again.

Spike was first petrified then relieved, thinking he was being attacked, then realizing it was Klocks' peculiar way of embracing an old friend. "Somebody's going to hear."

"They're all in town, probably eating Chinese. Chinese!" Klocks repeated bulging out his eyes, still in a state.

"Klocks, you scared me." Then Spike loosened up. "Owllleeeey," he yelled back at Klocks, overturning him and wrestling him to the ground, until he had Klocks pinned and nearly suffocating.

"You win, you win," Klocks called out, genuinely overjoyed to see his old buddy in the privacy of the Adirondack woods and free of the prison.

They got up and walked inside arm and arm. Spike should have remembered there was no predicting Klocks. God, he didn't know what to think when he charged. Spike was surprised himself at how glad he was to see Klocks.

"Klocks, I got a plan, and it's good for both of us."

Klocks was back on his bunk with his head in his hands, quietly sobbing.

"What the fuck," Spike said, totally perplexed and baffled to see the Owl like this. That never happened in Troy.

"Ever since I pulled this off, I've been wacko, " Klocks said regaining his composure.

Spike pleaded, "Jesus, listen will you? I have a plan, and we don't have much time."

* * * *

Klocks listened intently, searching for nuances, signals of a trap, but after ten minutes, he began to buy into Spike's explanation of the Chinese logic. By his not showing, their Mafia woman had gotten off in federal court. Case dismissed. They were eternally grateful to Klocks, enough so they were willing to pay Spike to help him. They were smart enough to foresee that the longer Mr. Wallace hung around, the more likely he was to do something desperate and get recaptured. Then, the case would reemerge, and the feds would again put the screws to Klocks to testify.

"Shut up, Spike. I think you're right but for different reasons, and I want a cut." For a moment, Klocks was distracted by his previous ploy whirling through his mind. But he quickly decided. "I can't depend on Damian. That broad has him hypnotized. He's changed, and he better not cross me."

"Owlie, remember I'm still a guard. I'd just rather not hear this stuff. I'm way overboard as it is, with the Chinese and now with you. If you're with me Owlie, we'll work the cash out, but we got to run, we got a boat to catch, and a place to be by midnight." He paused. "I'm not even sure my running lights work. But look Klocks, you'll be heading south, anyway, out of the county. And maybe it's safe to go to Troy now. Your disappearance was in the paper down there too. You know one lady called you 'Robin Hood.' They quoted her in the Troy Record."

"I already know where I'm heading, and it isn't Troy."

"Don't tell me. We got to go."

"Not yet." Wallace Klocks was energized. Phase two was kicking in. He was stuffing the few pieces of clothing he had into his grimy, treasured bag, the same one that had tumbled half way down the 21 Mine. Klocks flipped the bag to Spike, and then swiped Damian's wool shirt off the hook before he ran out the bunkhouse.

"Where're you going?" Spike asked in earnest.

"I'm grabbing something before they get back. I need to send a message to those two."

"To who?" Spike yelled as Klocks ran toward the Main House.

"To everybody," Klocks yelled back, and then he said, "To Chantal, the slut that posed for the painting, to Damian, and to the Warden, yeah that primpy Warden."

Klocks tore in through the screen door on the back porch, though he could have gone in through the front door, they were all left unlocked during the day. He already knew that. But the front door was the Lincoln Pond Road, and some distant neighbor might drive by.

Above the barking of the dogs, which was like music to his ears, he strode right up to the granite mantelpiece in the living room, slid a cane chair over, stood on the seat, and removed Heidi's five foot long painting of a voluptuous nude woman and a tiger. He managed to race out holding the painting under his arm, knocking a piece of bracket fungus off the mantle, and sending the screen door clattering.

"I should have known something like this would happen," Spike said as he saw Klocks trotting back toward him with something big under his arm. As Klocks stepped up on the porch, Spike asked, "Why Klocks, why? Why complicate things."

"Because I'm an antique dealer. And some day this painting will be an antique. Besides, I'd like to be remembered. I like to plant little troublesome notions in peoples' heads, Hurricane. We all want our slice of immortality. I don't have kids, I only have victims to remember me by."

twenty seven

While Spike was up at the bunkhouse, Damian was down in Port Henry at Stewart's filling out an application, with Chantal by his side. When he finished. the manager read it over, made a crack about hiring an ex-con, and asked Damian for his neck size.

Damian hesitated. Chantal whispered, "It's for a shirt, see, "she said, pointing to the girls behind the counter, who were looking a little sheepish as they figured out they might be working with this guy.

"Fifteen and a half. A large," Damian said.

Chantal's friend, the manager, walked to the back room, rifled through a pile of shirts still in their cellophane bags from the cleaners and grabbed one.

"Here's a sixteen. That'll have to do." He tossed the burgundy and blue shirt with its Stewart's insignia to Damian. "You start Saturday night at six."

"Saturday?" Damian said haltingly.

"Is that a problem?" the manager challenged.

Chantal gave Damian a friendly elbow and somehow he got the message.

"No sir, that's fine. I'll be here right at six."

As they strolled on Main Street toward the Champ Hotel, about a block away, Chantal explained that Friday and Saturday nights were the hardest nights to fill and he'd have to put his time in, until he built up a little seniority. "At least you have a job," she reminded him.

"That's true." He turned the shirt over and over. He never thought a simple shirt would impress him. "How much does it pay. I forgot to ask."

"Probably minimum, $5.15," she said with some assurance.

Damian looked at her. "Would he have hired me, if you weren't there?"

"What do you think, sweetie?"

"How do you know him?"

"The way I know most men around here. I used to date him."

Damian shook his head in dismay, hating to be reminded all the time of her past.

"It's a small town and I grew up here and moved back here. That's a lot of time in a small town. But that's over with, honey. You're here now to make sure."

"We'll see," Damian said somewhat morosely.

They were passing the red sandstone steps in front of the Champ Hotel and Pete was standing with an artist's paintbrush in hand, carefully painting in the date of the most recent sighting of Champ.

"Mr. Damian Houser, good to see you after all the furor we've had around here. I understand you did know the fellow that escaped." Pete seemed genuine, just making conversation, so Damian and Chantal stopped to chat. Chantal loved being seen with Damian. on Main Street anyway. One of the loggers on his evening run to Ti Mill tooted his horn and Chantal gave a wave, "Hey Charlie," she mouthed.

"Another sighting, eh Pete," Damian said.

"It's the telescope, I tell you. It's available today, Damian. Go in, take a look. It's all set up out on the back deck, the verandah," Pete said with a twinkle. "Gimme a minute here, and I'll join you. I'll even bring you a beer."

Quite a change in attitude from the last time, but Damian appreciated Pete's friendliness, especially knowing that he would soon be working down the street at Stewart's.

"Go on in," Pete said, waving the paintbrush in the direction of the lacquered lobby.

Damian gave Chantal a look and a shrug and she responded with a, "Why not?"

The 21 Mine

They made their way to the verandah overlooking the lake, and Damian pulled over the same painted metal chair he sat in the first time he looked through the telescope's magnifying field of vision. Damian fiddled with the eyepiece, focusing while scanning the lake for anything interesting.

"I told you what I saw last time," Damian said to Chantal, who remained standing in the background, her back against the yellow, concrete wall.

Most people agree that telescopes 'bring distant objects nearer' and what Damian wanted, was to make distant things clearer. He wanted that telescope to repeat the feat of foreshadowing Klocks' hand rising from the depths. He wanted to accomplish with that telescope what Klocks accomplished with his mind. Like Klocks, Damian wanted to develop and decipher the blurry pictures in his mind.

The surface of Lake Champlain looked cold and black, and Damian saw only one sailboat far to the north near the Vermont shore. Nobody was bass fishing in Bulwagga Bay or under the Crown Point Bridge.

"Not much to look at," Damian commented. Chantal stayed quiet, seemingly absorbed in her red fingernails.

"There should be," Pete said with a jaunty step, carrying two Saranac beers over next to Damian. "This is Spike Taylor's day off and he always takes that Hacker Craft of his out on his day off. He's got the only one on the New York side of the lake. The other's across the lake in Basin Harbor. We zipped over there one Sunday for the Classic Wooden Boat Show. It's almost identical to Spike's, thirty feet long."

"You just listen. You'll hear that throaty rumble soon."

Pete twisted off the tops and handed Damian one bottle.

"I never thought I'd like beer."

"Welcome to the Adirondacks," Pete said as he clinked his bottle with Damian's. And, sure enough, as they took their first swigs, as the sun was setting, reflecting off the bridge, a key was turned, and the bellowing of a two hundred seventy five horsepower, inboard, Hacker Craft engine, reverberated from Velez's off the hills of Port Henry.

"Get ready, what did I tell ya!" Pete chortled. "He doesn't waste any time and that baby can move. It's one sporty boat."

Damian had his eye back on the eyepiece, adjusting the focus and the downward angle, since the boat was leaving below and beyond them, from the beach on the other side of the tracks.

"He should be coming around the pier out from under the trees, right about now," Pete said standing up himself to get a look.

As if on cue, the Hacker Craft thundered into view, its smoky stern low in the water with Spike standing slightly bent in the cockpit, holding the sports car steering wheel in one hand.

"He's always on time," Pete said smugly.

The topside of the varnished mahogany hull glowed in the light of the setting sun.

"I think he has a passenger," Damian said, " and there's something lashed to the deck."

"Let me see," Pete said, motioning Damian aside. Damian obliged and they switched seats. "You're correct. He does have a passenger. That's unusual. Well, at least it's a man. His wife will appreciate that. Now, that thing on the rear deck is a bit strange. He's got it lashed to the rear deck, wrapped in a sheet or something. It's blowing all over the place. By the time he gets to the bridge that thing will blow off."

Damian was impatient to get his eye on the circle of view before the boat was out of sight, or it was too dark. "Pete, what do you say, my turn."

"Just a minute, mister. You'll get your turn on the way back. He takes a spin out to the bridge and back. He loves to show off. He'll be back."

But the echo of Spike's boat just faded away like the setting sun and pretty soon the three of them just stood on the verandah, silently watching, Chantal with her hands clasped behind her head. looking awfully sultry, waiting for this scene to end.

Spike didn't come back. "Sorry, Damian. I don't know what to say. He always comes back. He must have gone south. " Throwing up his hands, he walked back out to the lobby with them. "At least you got one good look. Next time you see him, ask him. Now that you're working at Stewart's, you'll see him. He stops in there all the time."

The 21 Mine

Chantal and Damian were quiet as they walked back to her truck on Broad Street parked diagonally to the curb in her usual spot outside the Golden Palace.

"By the way, Chantal, how did he know I was going to work at Stewart's? Did you say anything?"

Chantal started the truck and with practiced ease whipped out in reverse and then roared up the hill back to the ranch. Then she answered. "Nope. It's a small town, Damian. That's all I can say."

Jeff Kelly

twenty eight

The disappearance of Klocks had changed Warden Adiaz DeJesus. It had shaken him and his stature in the prison bureaucracy that fanned out from Albany. Officially, Wallace Klocks was dead. The assumption was that in the inmate's desperate state in the unstable environment of the 21 pit, Klocks had fallen down one of the shafts and drowned. That was the official story. After all, the searchers found his boot; they found his sock, his footprints and his blood all leading to a precipitous shaft in the darkness of a tunnel.

Warden A. D. was certain calling off the search had been the right thing to do, and a month later the public and the press seemed to accept that decision. Some cynical Moriah souls questioned why no relatives or friends ever showed on behalf of Klocks, but then this escaped prisoner was known as a solitary soul. Others in the prison community, guards speaking anonymously, off-the-record, speculated about the witness-protection program. They knew he had been sentenced through the Detective Syndicate and was scheduled to testify in a federal smuggling case involving illegal aliens. Maybe the escape was staged, they said, and he was living in some suburban condo, under twenty-four hour surveillance for his own protection.

Publicly, Warden A.D. was convinced that Wallace Klocks was dead. He admitted, though, that an additional reason for calling off the search had been his worry about losing one of his men down a shaft and tarnishing his reputation even further. The Warden was a thorough man and behind the polished door of his carpeted office he had time to think and do his own research. He went back over all the files he had on Wallace Klocks, all available records. In his mind, he recalled his own conversations with Wallace. He even interviewed the librarian. Some doubts did arise. He acknowledged that Wallace had researched the 21 Mine, but given the overwhelming evidence, he felt justified in concluding that Klocks was dead, drowned somewhere in the abyss of the 21 Mine. It wouldn't be the first body the 21 Mine had claimed.

The incident, as it related to the warden and the prison, never ballooned into anything larger. Outwardly, the Warden didn't change any of his findings or opinions on the escape. He tried to close that book and focus on his retirement in two years to that beach in Puerto Rico. But, inwardly, the nagging doubt that there had been an escape on his watch entered the meticulous psyche of the Warden and was sabotaging his attempt at a perfect retirement.

* * * *

A.D. was writing his final summation, not the official report which he had mailed to Albany one month ago, but a personal log of his prison career. Thankfully, this was the only attempted escape he had to write about, but even one escape was one too many, and he was annoyed that his sparkling image was sullied.

He had just slapped the green journal shut, five weeks from the day of the escape, when the private line on his phone rang. It was Heidi, whom he had only seen once since the escape, asking if he would come over. Warden A.D. was pleased and they set up a date for that evening. Before he left his office, he glanced approvingly above his desk at Heidi's painting of a red fox.

The Warden drove himself and parked underneath the now-leafy, overhanging maple tree, effectively hiding his jeep. The less talk the better, he figured. He had contemplated wearing one of his golf shirts, but decided to stick to his new, dark brown suit. He took a look at himself one last time in the rear view mirror. He brushed off his right shoulder, jiggled his gold bracelet, and felt as if he were eighteen again, picking up a girl for a date.

The 21 Mine

As usual, Heidi had locked all three dogs behind the fence in the back yard. They still barked, but they would stop once they saw their mistress at ease. He headed for the door.

In preparation for this night, Heidi had been unusually fickle, and even unsure of herself. She tossed aside her blue jeans and picked out a dancing skirt, orange and black with bolts of blue through it. What the hell, she put on a black bra and unsnapped her white cowboy shirt an extra button. A little cleavage made a man more alert. She kept her hair in braided ponytails down the front.

She had one serious issue to discuss. But she knew too, that she just wanted to see him. Plus it was a Friday night. She smiled through her wrinkles and looked strong and seasoned, capable of curling a man's toes if need be.

She heard the knock, and purposely waited a few moments before pulling open the heavy, oak door. "Howdy Ma'am," he said playfully above the racket.

"A. D., how are you?" Heidi asked with genuine warmth. They rather politely embraced, kissed on the cheek and stood where they were, surveying the outdoors. It was a hot and windy June day, with no black flies. The dogs quieted, and for once he enjoyed simply standing outside.

"I saw an indigo bunting yesterday out on the pasture," Heidi boasted.

"What's that?" he asked, as he took his suit coat off and flung it over his shoulder.

"It's a bird, a brilliant, turquoise blue. It's the first time I've seen the male. Looks like it belongs in an aquarium."

A.D. stood quietly. He was preoccupied.

"You've been through a lot with that escape haven't you?" Heidi said.

"Please, it's over with."

"Not for the town. They're still talking about it. A lot of theories are floating around."

"So what," A.D. snapped. He was surprised at how testy he was. Just the name Klocks set him off. "I knew from the get-go, he didn't belong here. I'll admit I never had him pinned down. But my instincts were right."

"Come in. I have something to share with you," Heidi confided.

"All right," A.D. said with equanimity.

"Can I get you a glass of wine?"

"Absolutely," he said, his disposition growing sunnier. He was thinking that an evening like this was just what he needed.

This time he didn't head for the red, cushioned chair. Instead, he stood in front of the window, staring outside. Accustomed to taking control, he asked, "How about some music."

"Of course. What would you like? Country? Soul?"

"What about the Four Tops?"

"You're showing your age now," she teased.

She turned and went into the kitchen and brought out a tray with two crystal glasses and a bottle of red wine. "Here, open this for us, while I look through my C.Ds."

"Fine, that's grand," A.D. said, bowing slightly as he took the tray from her. He thought they were on the same page and the evening held promise. He wore his gold wedding ring, but sensed she didn't care.

No Four Tops, but Heidi found a Miracles' C.D. The first song was "Going To A Go-Go." She turned the volume low, so they could talk. Background music.

"Cheers," A.D. said. They held up their glasses and clinked. "Excellent," he said, after swirling the merlot in his mouth before swallowing. He was a confident man, but not quite confident enough to take her in his arms and kiss her right then. A few more glasses maybe.

She sat back on the corduroy couch with over-stuffed pillows, and so did he. She moved her hand toward the bottle on the scarred cherry wood table and then rather gracefully whisked away a carved wooden ashtray, but not before A.D. noticed the remains of a joint in it. He chose to disregard the roach and pass on reproof.

When he handed her the wine, her tone changed slightly.

"A.D., our agreement was for one of my fox pictures, which you've received, correct?"

"Yes, correct," he said, slightly annoyed, feeling that transaction was complete.

The 21 Mine

Gently, she touched his elbow and said, "I want to show you something." She led him over to the fireplace in the living room under the mantle. This time he was totally absorbed in her and not aware of the surroundings.

With a peculiar look in her eyes, trying hard to be discreet, she looked at him and then up at the long, rectangular blank space where her painting of a languishing nude woman and a tiger had once hung.

"It's gone. My most precious painting is gone. It's been almost a month now. I was hoping you'd know something."

Warden A.D. was flabbergasted and momentarily at a loss for words. "I'm sorry, but, where is the painting? I liked it, but I know what our agreement was. This whole escape thing has monopolized my time. Otherwise, I would have come over sooner."

"I'm not saying you took it," she said in a pleading voice, her face close to his. "But frankly, I wish you had."

"No, I don't have the painting," he said gently, unaccustomed to a comforting role, but not quite adept at responding to this woman he admired and had dreamed of possessing. "And I don't know anything about it." He sipped the wine. "I liked it. That's the one your daughter modeled for, right?"

She threw up her hands, backed up and threw herself down on the couch. "I'm sorry. I thought for sure you'd know something about it." She was upset. "That means it's been stolen."

There she was sprawled on the couch, but for the wrong reasons. The Warden let out a long breath. He headed for the familiar red cushioned armchair across from her, and gulped the wine as if it were a shot of whiskey.

They were both silent, dejected.

"You'll have to report it to the police," he said. "At least you can collect insurance." He immediately felt dumb, just inconsiderate for saying that. He could see that was the farthest thing from her mind. Above the mantle remained the dusty outline of the discolored wall, a haunting reminder of where the painting had once hung.

Finally, she sat up. "I can't call the police."

The Warden waited patiently.

"I can't call the police, because I think my daughter knows who took it. She and her love sick puppy might even have had something to do with it."

"Damian Houser? All I've heard is good things. He's still working at Stewart's. Now my guards stop there for coffee, instead of the Rexall. They have more in common with Damian," he said, raising his eyebrows.

"I should have never let him work here, A.D.," she said, pointing her finger at him. "I like you, but I told you, didn't I? Down at the high school years ago, I warned you."

"Heidi, please, you're upset. And Damian didn't escape. He was released."

"I know that. But he wouldn't have been here if your damn prison wasn't here."

"Now hold on, what makes you think your daughter and Damian are involved?"

She was near tears. "Because she's been acting strangely lately, and she's hanging out with an ex-con. And, the painting disappeared eleven days after your monster Klocks escaped into that bottomless pit."

"What date was the painting taken?" the warden asked, his mind starting to turn.

"There's more. That inmate of yours, Damian, plans to buy John's blue Cadillac. Five thousand dollars! Now where is he going to get that kind of money. Stewart's? I don't think so. Chantal doesn't have that kind of money. The car's a classic, in perfect shape, and I know he wanted five thousand for it."

The warden was pacing the floor now, concentrating.

"Klocks stole paintings, usually old ones."

"I didn't say anything earlier, because I don't want to get my daughter in trouble. The timing just isn't good." She sat up. "A. D." she whimpered, "I think someone else besides Damian stayed out at the bunkhouse."

"Why do you say that?" A.D. asked, very business-like.

"Because one night when they were both in town getting ice cream," Heidi was trying to recalls things accurately. "I saw the light of a candle flickering through the bunkhouse window. Now, it's possible Damian could have left a candle burning, but I told him not to. He was good about that. And with Chantal there, she's petrified about fire. She would never have let him leave the candle burning."

"Oh God, Oh God," the Warden said in a barely audible tone, as he started to pace the room. "I don't like this." Klocks' files were popping back up into his head. Wallace's penchant for stealing paintings. His past association in prison with Damian. The two of them working here at her ranch. "Christ, no, it can't be," he whispered, under his breath.

"Do you mind if I help myself to another glass of wine?" A.D. knew he had been under a lot of pressure since the escape. Maybe I'm stressed out, jumping to conclusions. 'Calm down,' he told himself.

The Warden tried to slow the direction of his thoughts. The implication that Klocks might still be alive confused him. Finally, he said aloud, "That's nonsense. That's impossible."

Awkwardly, he looked over at Heidi as the warmer emotions toward her were overshadowed by a growing uneasiness. "Listen, I do feel partially responsible for what's gone on here. I didn't remove the painting. I don't know who did. Frankly, now you've got me worried."

"I don't want my daughter implicated in anything," Heidi said

A.D. was thinking. Nothing to be gained, he said to himself, and then out loud. "Heidi, there's nothing to be gained by this speculation. You think it through. There's no good that can come out of this for you and your family, or for me. Nothing. Don't speculate. Kiss the painting good-bye."

He sat opposite her and put his hands on her shoulders. Their heads down, they gently bumped foreheads. "Good for Damian if he saves enough money to buy a Caddy. Who cares? He's the first inmate I know of to stay in the Adirondacks. I'll tell you something, dear; I won't be staying here forever. I'm going to where it's a sunny day in June every day of the year. "

"You know what I say, run some electricity out to that cabin, dress it up a little, and let the two of them live there. The community is getting used to Damian. Everyone likes him; that's what I hear. That's what Hurricane tells me. Who knows, maybe you'll get some grandchildren out of the deal."

"Okay," she whispered, as she moved her hands up his arms around behind his neck. "I had a painting stolen. One painting. I should leave it at that, right?"

"Right," he said in an intimate tone as the hands on his neck sent a tingling sensation down his spine. He hesitated. Their heads were so close they could smell each other, and their eyes were closed. She didn't even hear his last word. She kissed him softly and slowly on those thin lips of his, but he didn't respond in kind. He was shaken, overtaken by a troubling daydream that was to haunt him for the rest of his days.

He saw Klocks in a ramshackle antique shop somewhere on the coast of Florida. Maybe in the Keys or the Panhandle. Klocks was making his living under a new name buying and selling antiques. Across the length of the back of that shack, above a collection of geodes together with a sparkling chunk of iron ore which wasn't for sale, hung a painting of a nude woman lying with a tiger. Klocks stood smiling behind a glass counter, eager to please his next customer.